MVFOL

HEAVENLY

"You need not answer." Valen swore under his breath. Now he was the one confused. "It was a foolish question. I will take you back to the manor now."

He jumped down from the wall and held out his arms to her. Elizabeth slid trustingly from the wall into his embrace. She didn't leave her hands on his shoulders. Instead, she entwined them around his neck, resting her body against his, and whispered huskily in his ear, "Yes."

Then she sought his lips, and he thought perhaps heaven had descended upon him, so sweet was her kiss.

BOOK YOUR PLACE ON OUR WEBSITE AND MAKE THE READING CONNECTION!

We've created a customized website just for our very special readers, where you can get the inside scoop on everything that's going on with Zebra, Pinnacle and Kensington books.

When you come online, you'll have the exciting opportunity to:

- View covers of upcoming books
- Read sample chapters
- Learn about our future publishing schedule (listed by publication month *and author*)
- Find out when your favorite authors will be visiting a city near you
- Search for and order backlist books from our online catalog
- Check out author bios and background information
- Send e-mail to your favorite authors
- Meet the Kensington staff online
- Join us in weekly chats with authors, readers and other guests
- Get writing guidelines
- AND MUCH MORE!

**Visit our website at
http://www.kensingtonbooks.com**

Cut From the Same Cloth

Kathleen Baldwin

ZEBRA BOOKS
KENSINGTON PUBLISHING CORP.
www.kensingtonbooks.com

ZEBRA BOOKS are published by

Kensington Publishing Corp.
850 Third Avenue
New York, NY 10022

All Kensington titles, imprints and distributed lines are available at special quantity discounts for bulk purchases for sales promotion, premiums, fund-raising, educational or institutional use.

Special book excerpts or customized printing can also be created to fit specific needs. For details, write or phone the office of the Kensington Special Sales Manager: Kensington Publishing Corp., 850 Third Avenue, New York, NY 10022. Attn. Special Sales Department. Phone: 1-800-221-2647.

Zebra and the Z logo Reg. U.S. Pat. & TM Off.

First Printing: March 2005
10 9 8 7 6 5 4 3 2 1

Printed in the United States of America

Chapter 1

Weaving Dark and Light

Valen, Lord St. Cleve, stood at the foot of his father's bed, clutching one of the massive posts. Like a chiaroscuro painting, the candle on the bed table illuminated only one side of his father's face as he lay on his pillow, eyes closed, sagging skin pale as unbaked bread.

His aunt's gown rustled as she rose from a chair and came to stand beside him. "He's not well today, I'm afraid."

"Well enough." His father blinked against the candlelight, squinting at Valen. "So, my errant son finally paid a visit, eh? That is you, isn't it?"

"Yes." Valen shifted uncomfortably.

"Come here, boy. I want another look at you before I leave this veil of tears."

Valen moved slowly into the orb of flickering candlelight.

"Not up there." He coughed. "Like peering up

at Goliath. Sit down here, where I can see your face."

Valen complied hesitantly.

His father nodded almost imperceptibly, smiled, as if satisfied in some deep part of his soul, and sighed. "You've the look of her. Your hair. Like fire. Golden one minute. Red as embers the next." He rested for a moment, then pursed his dry lips and tugged at the course linen of Valen's shirt. "But what's this? Wandering about the country in your undress again?" Even in his sick bed, Valen's punctilious parent wore a blue silk coat with a lace shirt underneath.

Valen glanced down at the cambric shirt he wore untied at the throat and flicked one of the dangling laces. "Riding. And hardly naked, my lord."

"Ha." His father snorted and settled back to study Valen through narrowed eyes. He closed his eyes a moment later, but resumed speaking as if the combined labor was too much. "I've somewhat to say to you. Ought to have said it long ago. Didn't. Then, you went haring off to that confounded war." His eyes flew open. "I thought I'd lost you."

"Hardly. It would take more than Napoleon to do me in."

"Reckless!" He snapped. "A foolish risk."

Valen didn't answer. This wasn't the time for old petty arguments.

"Title. Land. All lost if you had died."

"You've other heirs."

"Brothers, nephews." He balled a feeble fist and struck the bed beside Valen's leg. "The land is ours, boy. I see through this care-for-naught gambit of yours. Doesn't fool me a bit. I know you love every gully, every stalk of grain . . ." He gestured weakly at the drawn curtains. "Every flea-bitten sheep out there."

There was nothing to say. It was the plain truth.

His father nodded and relaxed. "I'm glad you're back. It fares better in your hands than ever it did in mine."

"You're still lord of Ransley Keep."

His father closed his eyes and made a soundless chuckle as if Valen had jested. The effort made him cough—a violent spasm, racking his frail body so hard that Valen leaped up to help raise him from the pillow. The old fellow held a white silk handkerchief over his mouth. Impossible to miss the blood staining it after the coughing spell subsided. His father fastidiously straightened the sleeves of his bed jacket, fighting to regain his composure.

Valen judged the interview had gone on too long. "You summoned me. I pray you, do not leave me quaking with curiosity any longer. I am your servant, my lord." He inclined his head.

"Very prettily said. One might almost think you were not mocking me."

For a tenuous moment, they sat in silence, gauging one another. His father inhaled deeply. "I'm about to stick my spoon in the wall. You"—he jabbed a finger in the air at Valen—"will be alone. This time, I'm leaving. No one will be left for you to bedevil. If you run off on some foolhardy escapade, you won't be punishing anyone but yourself."

Valen didn't like the direction the conversation appeared to be taking. "Now there's a quandary. Perhaps, I shall be forced to take up bedeviling Aunt Honore."

Honore thumped him on the shoulder. "Oh, do be serious."

"I am always serious."

"Ha! Hardly." She arched her brow. "Impetuous, I would say, and obstinate. Rather like your grandfather." His aunt knew how to fly straight down a man's throat and claw out his liver.

Valen flexed his jaw before composing his answer. "If I knew precisely which pint of blood I owed to that pompous old goat, I would gladly open a vein and drain it out."

"He was not an old goat." She glared at Valen. "You never knew him."

"I never wished to."

"Stop!" His father wheezed.

They abandoned their quarrel.

Lord Ransley propped himself up on one shaky elbow, wagging his finger at his son. "That's the point. It's over. Did you think I never suffered for not standing up to him? And your mother . . ." He collapsed back against the pillow and closed his eyes.

Valen studied his father's hand as it lay flaccid against the bedsheets, bulging veins pulsing erratically under the translucent skin. He looked away, squinting up at the murky dark corners of the ceiling where death hovered.

Lord Ransley took a deep breath and threaded up more words. "Hear me out. One request." He paused, his chest rising and falling as if he had just run up three flights of stairs. Despite his struggle, he gazed steadily at Valen. "Find a wife. One you can love. Have children. Not just to carry on the wretched title, but to occupy that unruly cavernous heart of yours."

Valen struggled to remain calm. "That, sir, is more than one request. Indeed, it sounds as if it is a lifetime of requests."

"Nevertheless—"

"Very well then, if you insist. I'll take the milk-maid. Shall I? Oh, but no, we know how that old story goes, rather too sadly. What then? The London Season? All the finest little peahens ready to strut past and lay down the goods for money and a title?" He stood up and raked his fingers through his hair, scraping the wild mess back from his forehead. "I don't know how you can possibly expect—"

"Nevertheless, I do expect it." His father waved his hand dismissing any arguments. "It is my wish."

Valen tempered his voice. "You're tired. We will discuss it tomorrow." He turned to go, but Lord Ransley grabbed his arm with surprising strength.

"There may be no tomorrow," he wheezed. "If God permits me into heaven, I shall hold your mother's hand and we'll look down on you with joy. Try to understand. You're the best part of our lives. Find a wife, son. Make a child who can fill your heart with hope." He glanced up at Valen. "And dread." He let go and fell back against his pillows.

In the silence, Valen's heart turned into a cannon-ball careening down his middle, crashing into his lungs, thudding down on his stomach. "Damn," he whispered, flexing his jaw. Too much. It was all too much. He'd come home. That should be enough.

He backed toward the door. "If this great peal you are ringing over my head is any indication of your health, I don't expect to hang crepe this age. You should be resting instead of sermonizing me. I bid you good night, Father. I'll come to you in the morning, before I ride out, to see if you have any more grand requests to make."

He strode out of the room feeling like a great awkward giant. In the hallway, he thumped his forehead against the wall. His fists tightened into useless hammers. Every muscle in his body tried to pull itself inward. *What good is it to have a man's body, a man's mind? And yet, crumple like a child.* He cursed again.

"Drink this." Aunt Honore's voice drifted from the open door.

"Did you hear him?" the old man wheezed.

"Of course, I did. I'm not deaf."

"He forgot himself. Called me—" He chuckled softly, falling into another coughing spasm. "*Father.*"

Valen frowned. So, he had. And it had not been nearly so painful as he had anticipated.

One month later, Valen stood at the bottom of Lady Alameda's, his Aunt Honore's, marble staircase in Mayfair, waiting for her to descend. He relished her expression, when, at last, she joined him in the entry hall.

The nearer she came, the wider her eyes opened. "Surely you jest?"

Valen adjusted the lace at his sleeve. "I never jest."

"Then have a closer look in the mirror. You look a buffoon." Honore planted her hands on her hips. "A rather large buffoon at that."

"Really?" He glanced down at his trousers in mock confusion. "I was quite pleased with the effect."

"Rubbish! I've never seen an ensemble more at odds with itself and its wearer. Ghastly. I vow, I never even noticed you had freckles before seeing you in this awful shade of—" She tweaked the sleeve of his coat. "What is it? Dull gold or dung green? These lapels, Valen. Large enough a goose might use them to flap around with. It's an atrocity. Your valet ought to be drawn and quartered. I'll sack him straight-away."

"Don't have a valet."

"You do. I distinctly remember hiring one."

"Had to send the poor fellow packing. Kept crying like a babe every time I disagreed with his choice of coat. Or, for that matter, the choosing of any garment. Stumbled across a fellow from my regiment the other day. Hired him for the job."

"A soldier! Now see here, Valen. This is London, not some muddy battlefield. You need someone who—" She stopped, and narrowed her eyes at him. "Oh, I see. Having a bit of fun, are we? Poking your finger in society's eye? Throwing down a challenge for Brummel and his ilk, eh? Silly me. Here I thought you were in London to find a wife?"

"So, I am." His voice held a sharper edge to it than he had intended.

She tilted her head. "Precisely what sort of gel did you intend to attract? A lisping little dodo bird?"

"Perhaps someone who is not blinded by ridiculous fashions."

"More likely, a young lady who is blind altogether," she sneered.

"You have your stratagems, Aunt. I have mine. Shall we arrive even later at Lady Sefton's? Or would you care to be on our way?" He held out his arm.

Honore crossed hers stubbornly and refused to budge. "What? With you looking such an outlandish fribble? I'm not at all certain I wish to introduce you." She tilted her nose upward. "Goes against my sensibilities."

Valen gauged her mood and launched his counter-maneuver. "Ah, but your sensibilities will stand aside, I think, for your brother's sake."

"Not fair." She pressed her lips together and frowned at him, staring hard, as if his plans were etched on his forehead and she might decipher them if she concentrated. At last, she sniffed and looked away. "He'd cock up his toes if he saw you rigged out in those gadfly togs."

He'd won. Valen tried hard not to smile. "No doubt. But, a *gadfly?* Hardly. Perhaps, you mean a *popinjay.*"

"Precisely!" She waggled her hand at his trousers as if she might wave them away.

He took her hand in his, calmly laid it over his arm, and patted it.

"This is lunacy." She fumed, but didn't pull away. "Madness."

He smiled fondly at her. "A family trait, or so I've been told."

She exhaled loudly and trudged beside him to the carriage and on to Lady Sefton's garden breakfast.

Lady Elizabeth Hampton held court in a lush garden, reveling in the attention the ladies were giving her. And the gentlemen, well, what could be more gratifying? Each one was like a piece of fruit set out for her inspection. This one was too fuzzy. This one not plump enough in the pocket. This one too old. She fanned herself gracefully and smiled. Everything was going exactly as she had planned.

Then, fate took an evil turn. A horrifying creature walked under Lady Sefton's rose-covered transom and Elizabeth nearly choked on her own saliva. Her fan fell from her fingers. As her courtiers scrambled to pick it up, she jumped to her feet to make certain she was seeing the interloper correctly.

For the briefest moment, she forgot herself and frowned. The voice of her former governess tapped Elizabeth's shoulder. *Frowns beget wrinkles. Ladies must refrain from such destructive expressions.*

"Egad," she muttered, losing control of herself entirely, after obtaining a full view of the problem.

Handsome Lord Looks-Like–A-Cherub handed her the fan. She took it and attempted to say thank you, but *Egad,* was the only utterance stumbling from her lips.

Her fingers closed around the exquisitely patterned silk of her overdress, and with her other hand she rapped the wretched fan against her thigh. "Impossible," she whispered.

An attentive young man, with hearing too keen, inquired as to what might be impossible. Elizabeth remembered herself, smiled genially at her swains and bid them excuse her. Their downcast countenances bolstered her spirits somewhat. They inquired what they might do for her. How might they ease her alarm? Elizabeth reconsidered her predicament. With four gentlemen circling around her, at least for the moment, she needn't flee Lady Sefton's gathering. Although she was taller than two of the gentlemen, she might hide quite admirably in their midst.

But, drat it all, I came here to be seen, not to be cloistered away in a remote corner of the garden. No, it won't do. I must think of a strategy. Where is my brother when I need him?

Lord Looks-Like–A-Cherub guided Elizabeth back to the bench under the walnut tree, expressing concern over her sudden pallor. Lord Pointy-Nose-But-Has-Thirty-Thousand-A-Year began reciting a poem to cheer her up. Sir Blah leaned against the tree and flicked at the windswept wings of his hair,

warning Pointy-Nose not to make a cake of himself. Elizabeth lowered her fan to her lap and smiled
up at them, trying to look maidenly and helpless,
while planning how to murder the monstrous oaf
who had ruined today's hard won entrée.

"You're very kind." She beamed at them. "What
a lovely poem." She fanned herself and lowered
her lashes in Lord Pointy-Nose's direction. "I daresay, you have completely restored my serenity." She
let her fan flutter to her breast. "How clever you
are to have committed to memory the entire son-
net." He reddened at her praise, and she felt certain he would call tomorrow morning. "I especially
enjoyed the part about the birds singing so sweetly."
Surely, in so syrupy a poem, the fellow had recited
something about birds.

Given this modest encouragement, he rehearsed
again the stanza about trilling larks and morning
dew. Sir Blah rolled his eyes heavenward. Thank
goodness, her brother charged into the circle and
interrupted the tedium.

He greeted the other gentlemen. "You won't
mind if I take my sister away for a moment, will
you?" At their protest, he reassured them. "I promise
to bring her back." He teased them for ignoring
all the other young ladies, who must surely be pin-
ing for their attention. Before long, he had the lot
of them laughing and giving her up without a second thought.

Nobody could refuse Robert. He was as genuine
and warm as she was calculating and hard, twins
and yet opposites. What she wouldn't give to have
his effortless congeniality, his naive confidence.
While she must laboriously study every social tactic
and female ploy available, Robert merely grinned

and wormed his way into everyone's heart. *The wretch.*

Robert pulled her to her feet and tucked her hand under his arm. When they were out of earshot, he leaned close. "There's someone you must meet. Absolutely first-rate fellow. Tip-top."

"That tells me nothing, Robbie. How many pounds a year?"

"No. It's not like that." Robert halted and turned to her. "He's my friend. That's the point, isn't it? I want you to meet him, not bag him and drag him home to bail us out."

"Oh, I see." Elizabeth glared at Robert as he continued down the path, tugging her along behind him. "Begging your pardon, but I thought we had a plan. A rather important one."

"*You* have a plan. I'm simply your dubious pawn, my dear. St. Cleve has nothing to do with all that. Best of men." They rounded a perfectly sculptured hedge. "Met him on the continent. I'd trust him with my— Ah, here he is."

She came face to face with the monstrous oaf and forgot to breathe.

Chapter 2

I'd Rather Be Dyed

Elizabeth had searched all over Piccadilly for this red silk. Smashed strawberry, that was what the shopkeeper called the color. A perfect red, embroidered with white lotus blossoms delicately outlined in black, with dark green stems, and leaves curled artfully in the background. Only one obscure length of the unique silk in all of London, and she had found it.

Immediately, she had visualized the possibilities. And she'd been right. The red silk, against a stark white bodice and underskirt was captivating. She'd used just the right lines, in a devilishly clever composition, forcing the eye to travel exactly where she wanted it to go.

Lord St. Cleve must have purchased the remaining fabric and created—not a waistcoat, which might have been within the realm of reason. No, some demented tailor had made it into a pair of knee breeches. He was a large man, well over six feet, it would be impossible not to notice those dratted red-flowered unmentionables.

Elizabeth frowned. If that wasn't disgraceful enough—he must don a mustard green coat, which made the breeches stand out even more. *Best of men, indeed!* He was a great gangling macaroni, who even wore his hair long like her grandfather used to do, pulled back, but without white powder. If Beau Brummell saw Lord St. Cleve's conglomeration, he would raise a fuss so loud that the atrocity would be broadcast in every London paper by morning. Elizabeth, of course, would be found guilty of fashion-treason by mere association. She wondered if it was too late to thrust herself into the bushes and hide there until everyone left.

Her brother nudged her. Lord St. Cleve bowed. This was the part of the introductions where she was supposed to smile sweetly and curtsey. That would mean wiping away the fury and disdain she knew must be clearly written on her face. *Hang it all!* He was accompanied by a countess, a lady whose widely known reputation bordered on dangerous. One simply could not afford to offend her by fleeing. Elizabeth could not fight six generations of good breeding. She curtseyed.

On the way up from her curtsey, she decided Lord St. Cleve should be invisible, nothing more than a young girl's nightmare. She smiled genially at Lady Alameda as if there were no other person present.

The countess turned to her nephew. "Why St. Cleve, how perfectly marvelous! The two of you appear to be a matched set." She fanned herself coyly.

Elizabeth felt the heat of her distress burning up her cheeks.

Robert laughed. "What are the odds! Did you notice it, Izzie? Captain Ransley, I mean, Lord St. Cleve is wearing the same cloth as you." Her brother slapped them both good-naturedly.

Did I notice? Are you completely daft? "Kindly refrain from calling me Izzie when we are in company." It was the only *almost* genteel thing she could think to say.

The corners of Lord St. Cleve's mouth played dangerously close to a grin at her expense. Elizabeth strained not to frown outright. She would not suffer a lined face for this cockatoo's sake.

The gigantic lout did not take her subtle warning. "It would seem we have the same tailor, Lady Elizabeth."

Robert chuckled again. "Oh no. Quite impossible, you see—"

Elizabeth pinched her brother's arm with some urgency to stop him from bungling everything. "What my brother means is, naturally, I don't employ a tailor. As a general practice, ladies require the services of a seamstress or a modiste."

"Ah." St. Cleve nodded as if such an elementary point rivaled illuminating instruction from Plato.

Robert nodded amiably. "As to that, my dear old fellow, you ought to have *your* tailor shot at dawn. Your ensemble leaves something to be desired. Never say you went to Mr. Weston for that coat?"

Lady Alameda fanned a little harder. "Exactly what I told him. Shoot your tailor."

Lord St. Cleve did not appear abashed in the slightest by the criticism. "Heavens no. Wonderful little chap. Found him down by the docks. Works for a tenth of the price Weston demands."

"Claimed to be a tailor, did he?" Robert tilted

his head skeptically. "Do you suppose he might be blind?"

Lady Alameda covered the corner of her mouth with the tip of her fan. "I believe St. Cleve puts a rather high value on blindness. Do you not, my lord?"

The man remained impervious. "You mistake the matter. He's a perfectly fine tailor, most accommodating. Made everything exactly as I specified." He glanced at Elizabeth, waiting for her response, almost as if daring her to point out the glaringly obvious fact that a drunken sailor would have given the tailor more agreeable specifications.

She had no use for such nonsense. It was time to escape Lord St. Crazy's proximity. "Certainly, no one can fault your tailor's taste in fabric. It's an exquisite silk." She smiled and inclined her head with far more graciousness than she felt. "A pleasure to make your acquaintance. But now, I'm afraid we must be—"

Robert held her in place. "Izzie, wait, there's more. I was rehearsing to Lord St. Cleve our predicament."

"You what?"

Her heedless brother had the good sense to look at least a trifle chagrined. He adjusted his collar. "Yes, well, I explained most of it."

"Most?" It was almost a whisper. Her mouth went horridly dry. *Did he tell this mountainous fop the whole revolting tale? If so, we might as well grab a paddle, for surely we are headed up the river tick. After the rest of the* ton *gets wind of this, my chances on the marriage mart are over.* She collapsed her fan and gripped it tightly at her side. One of the tines snapped under the pressure.

Robert tried to reassure her. "He understood

the matter completely, and generously offered to help us."

Elizabeth whipped the fan open and began to fan herself in earnest, regardless of the flapping tine. *This is a nightmare. A nightmare.* She would soon awaken. Some wretched lark would be trilling something that would make more sense than her brother's incredible disclosure. "How?" she mumbled, her voice cracking under her mortification. "What exactly?"

"When I told him our address and about the modesty of our rooms, he and his aunt insisted we stay with them for the remainder of the Season. Didn't I tell you? The best of men!" He draped his arms around Lord St. Cleve and Elizabeth and patted them both warmly. "What could be better?"

What, indeed? She shook her head and managed a feeble smile of gratitude. She understood how Marie Antoinette must have felt when they moved her to the tower. Things were not going according to plan.

Chapter 3

Crawling through the Eye of the Needle

Lady Elizabeth felt like an orphaned waif sent to stay with wealthy relatives. She stood beside Robert in the white marble entry of Lady Alameda's enormous London manor house. It was breathtaking. Four towering Doric columns vaulted up several stories to a domed glass ceiling containing six oval windows, each adorned by paintings of naked cherubim. The walls were oyster white, simple, clean, understated elegance. A subtle plaster relief of Orpheus and the nine muses graced the wall opposite the staircase, and Grecian water bearers climbed the walls beside the marble stairs. As footmen unloaded their trunks and baggage, Elizabeth tried to appear staid and unintimidated.

"Extraordinary house." Robert gawked like a bumpkin. "Most generous of you, Lady Alameda, to invite us to stay. Can't tell you enough what a boon this will be."

Lord St. Cleve and his aunt smiled patiently at them. The lady inclined her head. "You must think of Alison Hall as your home for the Season."

Lord St. Cleve clapped Robert on the shoulder. "You are most welcome. Glad of the company."

Elizabeth noted that, apparently, Lord St. Cleve did not feel the necessity to extend his warm welcome to her. What did it matter? He was nothing more than an overly large, overly ripe leprechaun anyway: with that absurd waspish coat and apple green silk pantaloons, which although they were both green, did not compliment one another at all since the coat was a bottle green stripe. Making the entire outfit even more ridiculous, he wore a vivid blue waistcoat. All he needed to look a complete fop was to pouf out his overly long hair. Elizabeth sniffed, and caught Lady Alameda scrutinizing her.

"You are twins, are you not?"

Elizabeth nodded. "Yes, my lady."

"How odd." Lady Alameda tapped her cheek. "You don't look at all alike."

Surprised, Elizabeth and Robert turned to one another, assessing the validity of her comment. Elizabeth saw in her brother the same black hair reflected in her mirror every day, the same china blue eyes, and a slightly larger image of her own nose complete with the annoying bump in the middle marring its straight line. They were similar in almost every respect.

Robert nodded genially. "Oh, I see what she means. I am a full inch taller. I suppose that's what comes of being male and female. When we were babes, no one could tell us apart. The tale goes that Papa threatened to paint our names on our foreheads. Naturally, now that we are older, there's bound to be differences."

"You seem nothing alike to me. Hardly twins. Opposites, I should say. Rather like a guileless puppy." She gestured loosely toward Robert. "And a oh, Valen . . . What is the name of that night-hunting creature? Is it a marmot?"

Elizabeth sucked in her breath. She didn't know what a marmot was, but she felt certain it was an insult, no two ways about it. Obviously, the lady must have taken her into dislike. She had no idea how to respond.

Lord St. Cleve glanced briefly at Elizabeth and shook his head as if warning her not to say anything. "My dear aunt, surely you cannot mean a marmot? We have no marmots in England. They prefer the colder mountain climes. Frigid little creatures, you see."

Most definitely an insult.

He continued, "I saw one or two in the mountains of Europe. They look rather like a fat squirrel crossed with a badger and spend most of their days waddling down holes." He smiled genially at her. "Lady Elizabeth is far too noble a creature for such a comparison."

His elucidation failed to assuage Elizabeth's injured emotions, and she couldn't help thinking he had put several double meanings into his questionable description.

"A ground dwelling squirrel? Really?" Lady Alameda refused to let the matter lay. "I wouldn't have thought it. *Marmot.* The very word sounds so sleek and dangerous, as if it were a predator to be reckoned with." She winked at Elizabeth. "Not a mean, waddling, badger-like squirrel, surely?"

Elizabeth could not tell if she was being gammoned or if her character was being roasted and served up on a platter. Either way, she heartily wished to be somewhere else.

Robert nudged her. "Tell you what, Izzie. I'll trade you my puppy for your marmot. I'd much rather be thought sleek and dangerous."

With a wry grin, Lord St. Cleve tilted his head, watching her expectantly.

She took a deep breath as she struggled to find an effective rejoinder. When she could not, she gave up. "I will make you a bargain, Robert. You may keep your drooling puppy and take my waddling little marmot as well. I shan't be requiring either."

Lady Alameda smiled at her. "Well done. But it is too bad such a paltry creature bears that interesting name, is it not? Perhaps, in the dark of night, the wily marmot doesn't waddle at all, instead it leaps out of trees, falling upon unsuspecting rabbits, ripping them to shreds with its pointed teeth." The countess smiled cheerily at them as if discussing the merits of a fine piece of lace, rather than the violent and bloody demise of a hare. "It's possible. After all, one cannot always judge by appearances."

The very idea was so preposterous Elizabeth shook her head to clear it. *Vicious leaping marmots, indeed. Egad! We have moved in with a bedlamite.*

Lord St. Cleve flicked some lint off his green and white striped sleeve. "I believe you'll find that marmots would rather dine on flowers and grass than unsuspecting bunnies."

"Oh, Valen, do use a little imagination." Lady Alameda waved away his skepticism. "Entertain possibilities. Consider what might be." She directed their gaze to the ceiling with her spiraling palm.

"It is so much more fun than always staring through the peephole at what is." Her reverie drew to an abrupt halt and she clapped her hands together. "Now come! Let me show you to your rooms." She started up the circular stairs. "Lady Elizabeth, I have situated you just down the corridor from your brother."

As they headed up the stairway Valen waited, as was proper, for Elizabeth to pass. She couldn't help inquiring in a hushed undertone, "Your striped coat, my lord, it is very, er, unique. Does it signify membership in a club, perhaps, such as the Four-in-Hand Club, whose members wear the yellow and blue striped waistcoats?"

He glanced at his sleeves as if surprised to discover that it was, indeed, striped. "Why, Lady Elizabeth, how very astute of you to notice. You have guessed correctly. It signifies that I am part of a very exclusive assembly dedicated to protecting helpless, unsuspecting bunnies."

To give him credit, he delivered his reply with the utmost earnestness. So much so, that it wasn't until he developed a wicked smirk that she realized she'd been neatly trumped.

"We call ourselves the Marmot Hunting Club."

Elizabeth drew in a quick, sharp breath. Then she recovered herself, and sniffed as if someone had just fouled the air. "How odd, to form an organization to hunt a species that does not exist in England. You have my sympathy, my lord. It must be a very dull sort of club."

He appeared to be repressing an excessively evil grin. "Bound to pick up speed, we've just had word of a sighting." He grinned at her pointedly.

Elizabeth fought not to grind her teeth. *Ladies do not display their temper.* However, if it was true that a person could look daggers at another, she was giving it her best try, for she was completely non-plussed and could not think of an appropriate set-down.

Naturally, she did what she knew best. She stuck her nose in the air and flounced up the stairs, following after his insane aunt. Honestly, she began to wonder if Marie Antoinette didn't have an easier time of it in the tower, excepting, of course, the part about the guillotine.

That night Elizabeth hid in her room, taking supper on a tray, begging to be excused, owing to her exhaustion from the day's labors. It truth, she simply had no wish to subject herself to any further teasing and humiliation, and she was certain she would suffer precisely that were she to go downstairs. Elizabeth had a plan and she would stick to it. The sooner she accomplished her objective, the sooner she and Robert might remove themselves from this barmy purgatory.

Chapter 4

All Is Not As It Seams

The morning began by harkening back to deep winter. Gray mist seeped in around the casements, hanging gloom in the corners of the room with its chill fingers. Not a good day for a young lady to go for a stroll with her maid, and even less suitable for her to leave the house alone. Valen watched Lady Elizabeth leave Alison Hall from his upstairs window. She should not command his attention so thoroughly, but he could not remove his gaze as she glanced back to make sure she had not been seen. He knew what she was. She had evidenced it on that very first day. Uncanny that such an arrogant chit should be Robert's twin. A pity.

The corner of his mouth twitched upward. "The old long coat, Biggs. I'm going for a walk."

His former sergeant looked up from folding a pile of linen and glanced pointedly at the moisture collecting into rivulets on the windowpane. "Oh, aye, Capt'n. A glorious day for a stroll. And will you be wanting something to keep the sun off yer face?"

"Excellent thinking. The old brown hat with the wide brim."

Biggs moaned.

"Be quick about it, man. My quarry is getting away."

Valen had a fair notion where Lady Elizabeth might be headed with such furtiveness. She wore a dark hooded cloak as if she were merely a lady's maid on an errand. Clever girl. His worn brown coat marked him as a nobody—a person of no consequence. Ironically, she would look right through him, just as she counted on her own disguise making her invisible to members of the *ton*. He hurried down the stairs. The drizzle and fog made it a perfect day for a hunt.

Lady Elizabeth set a bracing pace toward the Strand, and seemed to know precisely where she was going. Valen kept a cautious distance, but had no trouble following her. Her height aided him on that score. When she crossed from St. Clements's church and headed down Water Lane there were very few passersby, so he had to be more discreet rounding each corner.

The establishment she entered stood in a row of crumbling brick warehouses, black paint peeled off the wooden first floor façade, new paint on the window proclaimed the inhabitants to be *Smythe and Sons, Purveyors Of Fine Goods From Around The World*. As he peered through the glass, he noted that Mr. Smythe looked neither old enough to have a son in business, nor young enough to be a son, unless the elder Smythe was a man in his dotage.

Izzie—he'd taken to calling her by Robert's pet

name when he thought of her, *a dangerous indulgence*—threw back her hood and spoke with animation to Mr. Smythe. Valen pulled up the collar of his coat and adjusted the brim of his hat, so that he did not appear too obvious as he watched them through the glass.

Smythe shook his head and gestured toward the bolts of cloth standing in bins against the wall. Lady Elizabeth, Valen schooled himself to remain formal when regarding her, shook her head vehemently. He caught bits and pieces of their conversation.

"Must be unusual . . . willing to pay." She plunked her reticule down on the counter. *Not a wise move, Izzie.* Valen caught the predatory gleam in Smythe's eye. The foolhardy chit would be lucky if the proprietor didn't knock her on the head and take her money without troubling himself to make an exchange. Without thinking, Valen wrapped his fingers around the hilt of his short sword, but Smythe did not make any untoward movements. Instead, the fellow excused himself and disappeared behind a curtained doorway.

Izzie glanced impatiently about the cluttered room. When her gaze wandered toward the window, Valen stepped out of view. A moment later, the sound of her muffled exclamation drew him back to the glass. To his great relief, she appeared to be exclaiming with delight over a bundle of shiny dark green fabric. And now, her effervescence would cost her top price. She should have restrained herself.

Izzie pulled three guineas out of her reticule and handed them enthusiastically to Smythe. Predictably, Smythe shook his head. Ah, as Valen suspected, after her effusive display the fellow would demand at least six. It caught him by surprise when she shrugged, put the three guineas back in her purse, and turned to go as if it were the end of the matter. Smythe was as nonplussed as Valen was. It had been obvious she wanted the cloth. Lady Elizabeth was not three steps from the door, and only four steps from discovering Valen peering in the window, when Smythe called to her retreating back. She stopped, but didn't turn. The merchant unrolled the green fabric onto the counter and called to her again.

"Three," she responded, with admirable resolve in her voice.

Much to Valen's surprise, Smythe acquiesced. Elizabeth turned and they began to dicker over the length of fabric.

Valen waited down the narrow road from the warehouse and watched her leave. The certainty in her step indicated she felt quite pleased with herself. He strode into Smythe's shoppe and slapped six guineas down on the worn wooden counter. "The fabric the young lady just purchased—I want the rest of it. And there'll be more blunt in it for you, if you send word next time she pays you a visit."

When the blighter began to hem and haw, Valen grasped him firmly by the collar. "I've neither time nor the patience to put up with your chicanery. Do you think I can't guess where that silk comes from? You'll do as you're told and be glad of the profit. Do we understand one another?"

Smythe nodded and wrapped the purchase in brown paper. Valen concluded his business in a matter of a few short minutes and hurried out to make certain Elizabeth did not meet with harm in this rackety part of town.

He caught up to her just as the drizzle began to let up. Following her home was something of a treat as he marked the determined lilt in her gait. No one would mistake her for a maid now, not with that aristocratic bearing. Lady Nose-In-The-Air Elizabeth would soon discover that she was not quite so superior as she imagined. He chuckled. Later today, he would have to bribe his tailor heavily to sew a very gaudy coat out of deep green silk figured with purple peacocks. Perhaps they might trim it with orange or yellow to make it sufficiently garish.

Lady Elizabeth turned when she heard his footsteps behind her on the stairs leading up to Alison Hall. Her lovely mouth formed an "O" as she took in his shabby appearance, weathered hat, and old brown coat.

She pulled back the large hood cloaking her face, and stammered. "Lord St. Cleve?"

Her shiny black curls caught the sunlight and for an instant, he had the mad urge to put his fingers in them. In the nick of time, he collected himself and tipped his tattered hat. "Lovely day for a stroll, is it not?"

"Yes," she answered uncertainly, water dripping from her woolen cape. "I enjoy a brisk walk before breakfast."

"Ah." He nodded.

She tried to tuck her package behind her so he wouldn't notice the lump under her cape.

He grazed his hand lightly over her shoulder catching a bit of water on his fingertips. "Bit of weather earlier on."

"So there was." She swallowed, uncomfortable under his scrutiny. "Nothing like a bracing walk, I always say. No matter the weather." She glanced about and stepped backward up another stair, toward the door. Her gaze landed on his package. "Out shopping at this time of morning?"

"I was hunting for something unusual. And you?"

"I told you, merely taking a morning constitutional." She frowned, bringing her full attention to bear on him. "You're dressed oddly. I wouldn't have known you."

"No?" He smiled. "Nor I you. Might have mistaken you for a lady's maid." He could not be completely displeased with the expressive way her brow crinkled up.

"A lady's maid?" Her voice had a bite to it. "What of you? To be frank, my lord, I should have thought you were a coachman. In point of fact, not a coachman, but rather a drayman."

He bowed. "At your service, my lady. But how rude of me to keep you standing on the front step when you are burdened down with a package. I will be happy to carry it for you. After all, what good is a drayman if he will not carry—"

"It's nothing." She quickly turned away and he watched a flush rise up her neck as she hurried up the stairs. "A trifle. I can manage."

At that moment, Cairn opened the front door and cleared his throat. The very correct butler admitted both of them into Alison Hall; apparently, their unfashionable appearance had not perplexed Honore's manservant. Valen reluctantly watched Izzie dash up the stairs to her room. He would've enjoyed a few more opportunities to goad her, to watch her lips purse together and her chin rise ever higher with each gibe.

* * *

Honore stood in the doorway of the breakfast room. "Not quite blind enough to the rigors of society, is she?"

"Not by half." Valen turned from watching Elizabeth's retreating form, allowed Cairn to help him out of his overcoat, and followed Honore in to her sunny breakfast room. A huge mural of the Roman countryside graced one wall. The windows on the other side were draped in butter yellow silk.

Honore resumed her place at the head of the table. "Still, she is a rather comely creature, is she not?"

"I hadn't noticed." He set his package on the end of the table.

"A gift for me?"

"Regrettably, it is not for you, my dear." He leaned down and kissed her on the forehead. "Something for my tailor." Unable to keep the corner of his mouth from curling wickedly, he turned quickly to the side table and placed a kipper on a plate.

"What is it? Hemlock?" Honore tapped the shell of her hard-boiled egg. "For I vow, if you are requiring him to make another set of clothing as revolting as the last, any self-respecting man of the cloth would prefer poison."

"Not a vicar, my lady, a tailor." Valen sat down with his plate heaped high. "And I've promised him complete anonymity."

She dipped her egg in salt and studied it on the end of her fork. "So, tell me, how is it you do not find Lady Elizabeth attractive?"

He had raised his knife, but now set it down with some force. "Are we back to that? I have not given the matter much thought."

"Why ever not? You get along well enough with

the brother. Her brother certainly approves of
you. Half the difficulties in a marriage are the re-
lations. You ought to know that much." She bit
into her egg and smirked at him while chewing.

He glared at her. Suddenly, the mound on his
plate seemed less appealing. "She is unsuitable."
There. That's an end of it. He raised his knife preparing to cut his fish.

"Eminently suitable, I should think. Did you miss
the intelligence in the eyes? Unless I miss my guess,
the gel can put more than two and two together."

"Which simply means she would make a suitable
chess partner."

"My dear nephew, you would be surprised how
often a marriage is like a chess match."

"Ah. Then I should marry a woman as dumb as
a post. For I wouldn't care to be beaten at the
game with any kind of regularity." He pierced the
fish to hold it steady. "Aside from that, Lady
Elizabeth has some rather unfortunate traits that I
find intolerable."

Honore tilted her head. "Unfortunate traits? I
hadn't noticed."

He glanced at her skeptically. "Don't tell me you
haven't observed how she holds her nose in the
air, as if the rest of humanity is far too malodorous
for a woman of her caliber."

Honore dipped the other end of her egg as she
mulled over the matter. "You are too quick to
judge. Perhaps, her nose was broken at one time.
Pushed out of joint, as it were."

He sawed his fish apart, refusing to give rise to
her ridiculous conjecture. He was not judging, he
was observing. Naturally, his aunt would prize
Izzie's intellect. She valued that trait above all else.
He, on the other hand, held to more sound stan-

dards. He thrust a portion of kipper into his mouth and chewed vigorously.

"I cannot recall the thing ever being broken." Lady Elizabeth stood in the doorway staring at him as though he had just slunk in from the sewer. She touched the tip of her nose. "Nor has it been wrenched out of joint. At least, not yet."

He stood up as she entered the room. The fish in his mouth turned to cotton wadding and he'd be damned if he could swallow.

"Cat got your tongue," she said softly, gliding gracefully past him as she went to greet Lady Alameda. "Good morning, my lady. I must thank you again for your hospitality. How very pleasant it is here at Alison Hall. So beautifully appointed. I daresay, I have not slept half so well since coming to London."

"You say you have never broken your nose?" Honore smiled at her with unabashed interest.

Valen dropped down into his chair. If he didn't drink something posthaste, he would choke on the wretched kipper.

"No," Elizabeth answered simply and without the least hint of self-consciousness.

Honore held out her hand to him. "There you have it, Valen. You were right. It must be the smell."

"Smell?" The vixen asked absently, while sniffing eggs and strawberries on the buffet. "Why? Everything smells delicious."

"I believe Lord St. Cleve is referring to the constant elevation of your nose."

Valen sent his provoking aunt a quelling glance and said firmly, "In point of fact, I was not referring to it at all."

His aunt, ever eager to bat about a hornet's nest, challenged his defense. "Oh, but you were. We were conjecturing as to the cause, were we not?"

He refused to be drawn in, but found himself compelled to stand and pull back Lady Elizabeth's chair for her. She turned to him before seating herself, the nose in question coming quite close to his chin.

"I suspect," she said to him, in a low cool voice. "You may credit my correct posture to the boards that were strapped to my back as a child, and the books I was required to balance on my head without letting them fall lest I wished a beating."

He felt an odd heat in his cheeks and his features must have softened, for she looked away, uncomfortable under his gaze. She turned brusquely and sat down. "I pray you, do not be so ridiculous as to pity me, my lord. It is thus with all ladies of breeding. We are carefully trained in matters of deportment and carriage. Is it not so, Lady Alameda?"

Honore lounged back in her chair, watching them with interest, munching very casually on a piece of toast. "Mmm. So I've heard."

Valen remained standing and dropped his napkin onto the table. "Pray, excuse me. I've pressing matters to attend to this morning." With that, he picked up his parcel and turned to leave.

Lady Elizabeth commented to Honore, "Lord St. Cleve has left a mountain of food on his plate. I fear I've put him off."

"Oh, I don't see how. I daresay, he's simply a finicky eater." Once again, his aunt had made an erroneous supposition.

There was, in his belly, an uncomfortable sensation that he could only be put down to hunger. It had, after all, been a long morning. But Valen would get something at his club rather than subject himself any further to the slings and arrows of two outrageous females.

Chapter 5

Knot in the Dark

Late that night, Lady Elizabeth sat in her room stitching by the light of three flickering candles. She had only two days to sew a gown for Lady Ashburton's ball, and she must accomplish the task without anyone in Lady Alameda's household discovering the embarrassing fact that she must act as her own seamstress. The Season pressed forward. High time she brought someone up to the mark, or all would be lost.

The intricate detail work she was putting into the bodice began to strain her eyes. Yet, it was necessary. The small tucks in the white crepe would create dozens of lines to pull the eye upward. Why so many young women fashioned dramatic creations for their flounces baffled Elizabeth, unless they wished to draw attention to their ankles or toes. Ankles might be well and good, but it seemed patently obvious which aspect of her anatomy most attracted the male eye. So, she focused on accentuating the bodice and left the hem fairly simple.

She heard a thud just outside her door. It was her brother, no doubt, stumbling home at this dreadful hour. She picked up a brass candle holder and went to the hallway, colliding with, not her brother, but Lord St. Cleve. "Good heavens!"

In the unsteady light of her lone candle, it took her a moment to note that her brother appeared to be draped around St. Cleve's massive shoulders. "Is shat my liddle Izzie Bizzy." Robert collapsed in a spat of giggles.

"Good heavens." She looked from one to the other.

Lord St. Cleve grinned wickedly at her. "You keep referring to the heavens, my lady. I don't believe this has anything to do with the sky, nor God's dwelling place. To the contrary, I do believe I've been cavorting through—"

She held up her hand. "You're both foxed."

Robert saluted her from his upside-down position. "Right you are, your highness."

Lord St. Cleve straightened under his burden. "*He* is foxed, madam. I have merely ingested too many glasses of watered down bourbon. There is a vast difference."

She raised the candle and stared at him. His neckcloth hung untied around his neck, his coat had gone missing and in the dim light, strands of his golden hair hung beside the hard lines of his jaw and shone red in the candlelight. There appeared to be nothing foppish about him. He looked altogether masculine. Frighteningly so. She stepped back, bumping into the wall.

"It's the smell, isn't it?" It caught her off guard

when, in complete violation of his character, he gazed remorsefully at her. "I'm afraid he retched on my leg during the carriage ride home."

Robert piped up. "Dem fine celebration. Too bad you weren't there, Izzie. Dunworthy came into his majority tonight. Fine fellow. Good family, even if they are Scots. Pots of money. Jus' yer type." He lifted his hand weakly in her direction. "Has a lovely sister, he has. Didn't you think so?" He twisted sideways attempting to speak directly to Lord St. Cleve and then gave up the effort. "Eh, Capt'n?"

"Lovely."

" 'Xactly. Yellow curls. Very fetching. Keen on you." Robert frowned. "Kept batting her eyes in your direction."

"You're blathering." St. Cleve turned to cart Robert down the hall to his room. "It's off to bed with you."

She held the candle aloft and led the way, opening the door. "If you will set him on his bed, my lord. I can manage from here." She hurriedly threw back the blankets.

Robert flopped onto the bed as if he was a sack filled with sand and had no bones whatsoever. She stared at her brother. "I've never seen him like this."

"I have." St. Cleve's hushed voice glided easily into a familiar place in her soul, as if they were old and intimate friends. "Once. On the continent— but that is another matter. Tonight, I ought to have dragged him away much earlier. Here, let me give you a hand with his boots."

Lord St. Cleve tugged off the boots, while she removed Robert's neckcloth, and struggled to shift him out of his coat. Half asleep, her brother mumbled grumpily and batted her hand away.

"Robert, for pity's sake. You cannot go to bed in your coat. You'll ruin it entirely."

The uncooperative slug rolled onto his side, muttering oaths at her. She gave up.

"It rained on us." St. Cleve stood beside her. "His coat is bound to be damp. We'd best take it off." Together they wrested Robert's arm out of the sleeve and rolled him onto his other side to remove the other.

St. Cleve handed her the sodden garment. "That should do. He'll rest well enough now."

She pulled the covers over her foolhardy brother and briefly smoothed back a few stray dark hairs from his forehead. Sweet, guileless Robert. If only she could count on him to shoulder more of the— but no. She would guide them through this predicament. Izzie turned and found St. Cleve watching her intently. "Thank you, my lord, for your assistance tonight. For bringing my brother home, and—"

"It's Valen."

"Valen?"

"My name."

"Yes, well, thank you, Valen." She retrieved her candle plate from the bed table.

He still stared at her. "You're fairly pleasant to look at. You realize that, don't you?"

She, who was accustomed to far more gratifying compliments, pursed her lips. "I am passable, my lord. And you, I believe, are foxed."

"I told you, call me Valen. For Valentine. Ghastly name. Never call me that. Just Valen. And I am not foxed. But you, you're in your night rail, and I can't help it, you are quite . . ."

She glanced down self-consciously and looked

up again, angry that he should mention it and make her feel foolish and indecent.

He snorted derisively and one corner of his mouth curled into an evil dimple. "I believe I'll take my leave now. You're about to let that tongue of yours loose on me. And I've had quite enough of it for one day, thank you, my lady."

Her grip on the candle plate tightened and her other hand balled into a fist. *Pompous lout.* "At least I do not corrupt naive young friends and stumble home in the middle of the night slinging insults at his sister."

He appeared to laugh at her and turned to go.

In a firmer tone she added, "If you think you've had a taste of my tongue today, just wait until tomorrow."

He stopped in his tracks and wheeled around, bearing down on her. "On second thought, I don't believe I'll wait until tomorrow." He clasped her shoulders and covered her mouth with his. He kissed her soundly, chastening her tongue quite thoroughly with his. Although, as chastening goes, it was rather pleasant. Startled, she failed to breathe. When he let go, she gasped. The candle, remarkably, still in her hand, wobbled uncertainly.

He said huskily, "You're right. I *must* be foxed."

She couldn't think. She put it down to lack of air. *Foxed? This is what he says after a kiss like that? Dratted man.*

She would have slapped him if he hadn't eased so efficiently out of range. "If you think I will accept, 'I'm foxed,' by way of an apology for this scandalous behavior, you are sorely mistaken."

"It was not an apology." He accented each syllable. "Simply a rationalization. I never apologize."

He turned and headed straight for the door, without so much as a by-your-leave.

Izzie fumed at his back as he disappeared into the blackness of the hallway. "Wretch."

She closed the door on Robert's room, and returned to her own with renewed zeal for her sewing. The sooner she brought Lord Pointy-Nose-But-Has-Thirty-Thousand-A-Year to the sticking point, the sooner she could escape Lord St. Rude-Uncouth-And-Overbearing. She decided to make the neckline of her gown a full inch lower than she'd originally planned. No more shilly-shallying about.

Not more than a half hour later, she heard scratching on her door. *Aha! The wretch has come crawling back to apologize properly.* Well, she wouldn't accept. She hurried to open the door, planning to ring a peal over his head he wouldn't soon forget. Her spirits fell when she saw it was a sleepy servant, his white wig askew.

"His lordship said to bring you these oil lamps, lest ye go blind stitching in the dark."

"Stitching? How did he—" She stopped and took the lamps from the servant. "Thank you. You may tell his lordship that he is mistaken. I am not sewing at this hour. However, I do enjoy reading late into the evening, and therefore, I will accept his offering as a gesture of apology."

The fellow glanced pointedly past her, at the sewing strewn across the small escritoire.

Izzie sniffed loudly. "Don't be impertinent. You will tell him exactly what I said."

He bowed. "Yes, mum."

She lit the lamps immediately and blew out her guttering candles. Pleased at the bright circles of light that illuminated her handiwork, she whispered, "Thank you." Although, she was uncertain whether she was thanking Lord St. Cleve, or the heavenly beings who occasionally made good things happen.

She bent back to her sewing, but before long, there was another scratch at the door. This time she approached it more warily. The same bedraggled servant stood in the hallway. "Begging your pardon, m'lady, but his lordship has sent me with a message for ye."

She tilted her head, holding the edge of the doorframe as she waited. "Yes?"

"He says," the fellow cleared his throat. "He says to tell the young lady . . . 'balderdash and folderol'!"

"Balderdash?"

"Yes, m'lady. That's it. Balderdash. And I was to add that it wasn't no apology. His lordship waxed rather course on the subject. Mentioned he'd rather burn in hell and a few other euphemisms what might be left unsaid, long as you take the meaning."

"Oh, I comprehend perfectly."

"Very good then." He bowed and tried to hurry away.

"Wait."

He turned around and trudged slowly back to her door, reluctantly awaiting her instruction.

"Folderol?" She repeated frowning.

"Yes, miss. I believe he was referring to the bit about you reading rather than sew—"

"I know to what he referred. You tell him . . ." But she could not think of how to respond.

The footman shifted impatiently from leg to leg.

Izzie tapped her finger against her lip, cogitating, and at last, she smiled. She knew exactly how best to punish the rascal. "You may tell Lord St. Cleve, that I do not wish to be disturbed any further tonight, for I am going to sleep, perchance to dream. And what will I be dreaming of? You may tell him, that I will be dreaming of the next time I might give him a *proper* taste of my tongue."

The servant stared at her warily.

She sniffed and corrected her posture. "Be sure you emphasize the word, proper."

"As you wish, m'lady."

And that, she thought, as she closed the door, ought to keep his lordship awake and pondering the direction of her meaning for quite some time. But neither did she go easily to her sleep, for she found her waking mind fixated upon the very dreams with which she had threatened Lord St. Provoking.

Chapter 6

Pattern Card of Perfection

Lord Pointy-Nose called on Lady Elizabeth the following afternoon. *Lord Horton,* she corrected herself. She must stop referring to him as *Pointy-Nose* in her mind. It would be disastrous if it happened to slip out in conversation. She scrambled through her wardrobe trying to find something suitable that he had not already seen, and almost didn't hear the scratching on the door. Elizabeth stopped her frantic search and jammed her hands onto her hips. If it was Lord St. Cleve's insolent servant sent to annoy her again, she would happily box his ears and say, "Take *that* back to his lordship with my compliments." Although, he was a burly sort of servant and she doubted he would take kindly to having his ears boxed.

Owing to the scant amount of sleep she'd gotten the night before, her patience hung on a short leash. With a deep breath, she schooled her features, reminding herself that she was a lady. No colossal jackass, be he a lord or not, was going to rattle her cage. Before she could order whoever it was to go away, the door opened and in trotted a maid that looked for all the world like a dwarf with a great bobbing topknot of brown hair piled on her head.

"Her ladyship sent this gown to see if it suits your complexion. She believes the shade will accentuate your dark hair and fair skin perfectly." She tipped up onto her toes and held some of the deep cornflower blue fabric next to Elizabeth's cheek. "And so it does. Her ladyship will be ever so pleased."

The odd little woman laid the gown on the bed and bustled about the room as if she were in charge.

"You're Lady Alameda's abigail, are you not?"

"Aye, that I am. An' seeing as you have a gentleman waiting downstairs, I expect you'll be requiring a bit of help."

Elizabeth obediently held out her arms as the lady's maid untied her tapes. "Am I to understand that the countess means to loan this gown to me?"

"Heavens no, milady. She wishes you to have it, with her compliments. She had it made for one of her nieces. No need of it now. Happily married, with a newborn babe. A lovely young lady. Saved my life, she did." The chatty maid went efficiently about her work, while relating a preposterous tale, wherein Lady Alameda's niece dove off a pier into a raging sea, and performed a daring rescue to save the maid from certain drowning. Her handsome lord found her on the beach and carried the young lady to safety. It had been years since anyone told Elizabeth a fairy story.

The gown slid over her shoulders, soft luxurious blue satin floating down, draping across her figure. The heart-shaped neckline curved perfectly over her breasts and fell in cunningly simple lines. Very plain, but elegant, it had been trimmed at the hem and neck with darker blue silk. Elizabeth vowed to study the pattern in greater detail when she had more time, for the effect was stunning.

She smiled and murmured, "It's absolutely brilliant. Lady Alameda is a genius."

"Oh, yes, miss, that she is. No question about it. Now, if you'll sit down, I'll be seeing to your hair, shall I?"

When Lady Elizabeth finally set her slippered toe on the white marble staircase and prepared to descend, it was with complete confidence that Lord Horton would be kneeling at her feet before the afternoon ended. Men were such simpleminded creatures. Most men. There were a few exceptions. Her inscrutable father for one. And Lord St. Cleve . . .

At the sound of his laughter emanating from the sitting room, she cringed. Once more, the lout was causing lines to form in her brow. No more wrinkles, she reminded herself. What she needed was a stiff plaster to hold her forehead smooth until the glorious day when she and Robert might remove themselves from Lord St. Cleve's abode.

More guffaws, louder this time, echoed from the second floor drawing room. Elizabeth recognized another familiar voice. Oh joy, Robert was there, too. The three of them were so effectively entertained they would neglect her entrance entirely. It was vitally important that Lord Horton receive a stirring impression. She hesitated on the stairs.

Cairn appeared out of nowhere and bowed. "Would you care for me to announce you, my lady?"

Yes. No. It would be doing it up a bit too much. She shook her head and stood in the doorway doubting whether any of them, Lord Horton in particular, would notice her at all. So much depended on her attaching his affections. The voice of uncertainty taunted her, whispering truths she didn't want to hear. She was a pauper and no real beauty in the bargain, merely a cunning craftsman, a trickster. What was she playing at? Her family's future depended on her, and what did she have at her command? *Precious little. A title and a few artful tricks.*

She vacillated between anger and tears as she watched the men laughing together. It was all so abominably difficult, and unfair. Robert failed to grasp the gravity of their situation. How could he stand there hooting like a schoolboy and slapping his friends on the back as if he hadn't a care in the world, when she must do this wretched marriage thing? Her hands began to shake, so she pressed them against her thighs. She would not succumb to nerves.

St. Cleve noticed her first. He abruptly stopped chuckling, straightened, and let go of the fireplace mantel, staring at Elizabeth with the same startled intensity he had the night before. She felt utterly naked under the broad strokes of his gaze.

He reddened. And so he should. However, she failed to understand why his features then hardened, and he frowned at her as if she had caused him some offense. Following such a shameless perusal, she was the one who ought to be offended.

"Ah, Izzie. Speak of the devil . . ." Robert gestured broadly to her. "I was just telling St. Cleve and Lord Horton about that time you put together a pair of wings for each of us."

She remained in the doorway exchanging hostile glares with Lord St. Cleve, refusing to look away until he did. She noted his coat was sewn out of a fabric very similar to the dark blue with which her dress was trimmed. Her glare took on a slightly triumphant twist. A coxcomb cannot appreciate having his feathers mimicked. Although, he did not look much like a coxcomb today. The blue coat was not so very extraordinary, and with his reddish gold hair, not entirely unflattering—she forced herself to look away.

Her brother was yammering on about something. It nipped at her sensibilities. "You told them what?"

"About the wings. You remember. The day we jumped off of the roof into the hay wagon."

"Surely you didn't."

Lord Horton came forward taking her hands in his. "A delightful story, Lady Elizabeth." He led her into the room. "I only wish I could have been there to see it. Your resourcefulness astounds me. However did you create the wings?"

"Robert, dearest . . ." She tried, ever so hard, to smile. "Of all the stories to tell—"

"Nonsense, Izzie. First-rate story. Tell them how you made the wings." Robert turned to St. Cleve and explained, "Our governess read us the story about the Greek chap and his father who made wings out of wax and flew too close to the sun."

"Icarus," St. Cleve muttered, his gaze flitting to hers and then returning to the fireplace mantel as if there was something of great interest on the naked surface.

"That's the fellow." Robert nodded gleefully. "So, our Izzie wonders what would have happened if he hadn't made them out of wax. 'Why not make them out of cloth?' she says."

"Why not, indeed?" Lord St. Cleve sounded cool and skeptical.

Elizabeth wished her vociferous brother would choose a different topic. She pulled on his arm as discreetly as possible. "We were ten, Robert. No one wishes to hear that silly old antic."

"Eleven. Oh, but Izzie it was marvelous. I'll never forget the way you soared off the rooftop. I honestly thought you were going to fly. Truly fly. And you did for a minute or two!"

"Hardly." She had their attention now, but it was not for the reasons she had hoped, not alluring beauty, or entrancing grace—the things men valued. No, she had their attention because she had behaved like an idiot, climbed out of the attic window, put on a pair of willow-whip and silk wings and jumped off the roof. "I suppose you mentioned how it all ended?"

"Not yet. Told them about me, falling like lead ballast into the hay wagon. Mind you, that was after I saw what happened to Izzie. Wasn't sure I wanted to chance it, so I just jumped."

Lord Horton lifted her hand and solicitously patted it, shaking his head. "It's a wonder you weren't killed, my dear. A wonder."

Robert eagerly drew them back to his dratted story. "That's the thing of it. Those wings she made were quite remarkable. She missed the hay wagon entirely. Sailed clean over. Wasn't until she tried to flap, things went sour."

Lord St. Cleve's mouth quirked sideways. He'd left off concentrating on the fireplace. "And then?"

Lord Horton leaned closer to her. "Yes, Lady Elizabeth, you must tell us all. Were you injured?" He still held her hand, as if holding it might save her from the disastrous results of a child's flight twelve years earlier.

She tried to smile charmingly, but Lord St. Cleve's smirk made it quite impossible. "Bruised, but otherwise in one piece."

Robert laughed and Elizabeth knew, short of gagging him with his cravat, there would be no way to keep him mum.

"The tree, Izzie. You're leaving out the best part. Tell them about the tree. And Father. It was spectacular. She glided straight into the old beech, the upper branches snagged her like a wayward cherub. Everyone on the estate gathered under it. Mother was terrified you were going to fall. Cook sobbed as if you were already dead. The stable lads laughed so hard they rolled on the ground, and Father sacked the governess on the spot. Surely you remember?"

"I was tangled in the branches. Rather busy at the time."

"Well, you can't have forgotten Father. As I remember he threatened you with a horsewhip if you didn't come down straightaway." Robert laughed as if it were a grand joke of some kind. And why shouldn't he? He'd been a son, second in line to the title, a boy, not a recalcitrant daughter.

Elizabeth recalled, all too well, their father's livid face as he shouted up at her. She'd clung to the branches, wondering if she might not be better off falling to her death rather than climbing down.

He hadn't used a horsewhip. It might have been better if he had. A thick willow bough had served the purpose. Father surmised who'd constructed the wings and led one of his heirs up to the roof. He applied sufficient persuasion to her back and legs to convince her to think more clearly in the future. After that, she had been consigned to studying household management and endless lessons on deportment and proper etiquette, no more history, or poetics, no more myths about Greeks flying too close to the sun. *No more foolishness.*

Lord St. Cleve broke into her stream of memories. "For pity's sake, Horton, stop chafing her hands. It isn't as if she's fainted." He appeared perturbed. "The gel jumped off a roof. Not the fainting type."

Judging by his exasperation, Lord St. Cleve preferred the fainting type.

Lord Horton dropped her hand as if it were an ember. "No, no of course not. Such a harrowing tale, I simply meant to comfort—"

"A child's adventure." Lord St. Cleve moved closer to them, his voice a trifle softer. "Who hasn't dreamed of flying?"

"Yes, quite. Just as the birds do." Lord Horton eased her away from St. Cleve. "And knowing how much you enjoy birds, Lady Elizabeth, I've composed a poem in your honor. If you will come and sit on the divan, I will be pleased to recite it for you."

As Lord Horton led Elizabeth to the couch, she caught her brother and St. Cleve exchanging disgruntled glances. So, naturally, she encouraged her admirer. "What? Only one poem? But I do so enjoy your exquisite verses."

"Oh!" he exclaimed and pulled a collection of papers out from the inside of his coat. "In that case, I brought two or three it might please to hear."

She smiled sweetly at her brother and St. Cleve. "Won't that be a rare treat?" She was certain one of them groaned.

Lord Byron need not fear Lord Pointy-Nose-It's-A-Lucky-Thing-He-Has-Thirty-Thousand's poetic talent. If it were not for the fact that she needed him to come up to the mark, Elizabeth would have expired from boredom. As he droned on, she had fallen into analyzing the construction of Lady Alameda's superb gown.

She glanced up as Cairn walked quietly into the room with a small silver tray in his hand. The card was not for her. He presented it to Lord St. Cleve, who read it quickly, nodded, and pretended to return his attention to the pitiable poet. Elizabeth wondered what St. Cleve might be dwelling on, reasonably certain it wasn't the noble song of sparrows and bluebirds. Did he recall kissing her the previous night? Or had he drifted off to sleep and forgotten all about it?

Cairn returned to the doorway and cleared his throat. Elizabeth's overdramatic poet stopped midsentence, his arm in the air, pointing to some imaginary fowl, and turned with the rest of the room's occupants to greet newcomers.

"Mr. George Dunworthy, and his sister, Miss Susannah Dunworthy."

She was everything Elizabeth was not—a sweet

demure little lamb with hair the color of lemon rinds curling out from underneath her clever chip straw bonnet. *Definitely the fainting type.* St. Cleve was bound to approve. Not that Elizabeth cared. Heavens no. Why should she? She didn't. But she hated Miss Dunworthy anyway, just for good measure.

Elizabeth stood up to greet the intruders.

The girl curtseyed to her, low enough to appease the Queen Mother. It had, however, the annoying effect of making Elizabeth feel nearly as old and ugly as the great matriarch herself. Miss Dunworthy smiled shyly. "I'm *tho* very honored *tho* make your acquain*than*th."

Gadfrey! She lisps. Elizabeth momentarily forgot her manners and stared at her, as if the wicked little kitten had just scratched her cheek. *A contrived lisp, if ever I heard one.* The men drew closer to Miss Devious-Dunworthy, apparently loath to miss overhearing her next bashful, babyish comment. *Perfection.* Elizabeth plopped like an artless old prune onto the divan.

The minx turned to Lord Horton and apologized effusively for interrupting his poetry. At least, it sounded like an apology. The childish lisp garbled her words so badly they were scarcely intelligible.

Thank heavens Lady Alameda breezed into the room, trailing a lacy shawl draped over her forearms as if it were royal robes. "There's so many of you! Superb!"

Miss Devious-Dunworthy honored Lady Alameda with another dramatic curtsey and pouted. "I am *thr*ying so de*th*perately hard to convin*the* Lord Horton to fini*th* re*th*iting his marvelou*th* poem."

"By all means." The countess took her place in the large armchair beside the divan and waved him on.

Lord Horton struck a pose before beginning. "Upon the wing, the bluebird climbs." His voice resonated with emotion. "Her spirit soars up with mine. Up. Up. Up! Above the clouds and leafy places, above the soot and city's smut—"

"My dear boy!" Lady Alameda interrupted, thumping the arms of her chair. "We won't have that sort of verse in this house. Not with young ladies present. Shame on you!"

Poor old Pointy-Nose was at a loss. "Oh, but . . . Not what it means . . . I—"

Elizabeth's stomach twisted as she watched this man, her future husband, stutter helplessly. If he could not defend himself against Lady Alameda's patently ludicrous accusation, how would he fare against a genuine problem? *Drat this marriage business!*

St. Cleve tried to remedy the situation. "I think, my lady, you may have misunderstood Horton's meaning. He refers, I believe, to the filth in the air, do you not?"

Lord Horton nodded dejectedly.

Lady Alameda stood up. "I think not! His first line clearly described a ladybird climbing upon the fellow's wing." She smoothed out a long imaginary tuft of feathers at a rather suggestive height.

Miss Devious-Dunworthy gasped.

Lady Alameda shook out her skirt as if some of the smut had landed in her lap. "I think you can see the implications there, without me spelling them out any further." She smiled genially at Lord Horton, whose mouth hung open at an odd angle.

"But never-you-mind," she said. "I forgive you. After all, young men cannot help but have these kinds of thoughts."

Lord Horton turned an interesting shade of pink. For being a poet, he was surprisingly short of words.

"Oh, do not be so distressed." Lady Alameda rapped him on the shoulder with her fan. "You may return, when there are not tender ears present, and read your poem to me."

She held open her arms as if they were all her long lost children. "Now for some amusement. I've prepared a surprise for all of you. We shall have our tea on the lawn, alfresco style."

Miss Devious-Dunworthy clapped her hands excitedly. "How per*th*ectly deli*th*ful!" One would think she'd found a gold coin in the Christmas pudding.

"Yes." Lady Alameda stared speculatively at the girl. "It ought to prove a great deal more entertaining. And I've devised another surprise, as well. Come!" She waved them up. "Come see for yourselves."

Chapter 7

Flying Shuttles

If Elizabeth had to hear the devious kitten pronounce anything "per*th*ectly deli*th*ful" again, she felt as if her head might explode. Naturally, that was the very expression Miss Dunworthy used when she discovered Lady Alameda had devised for them a game of battledore and shuttlecocks.

A child's game. Elizabeth crossed her arms and went to stand under the shade of a large tree beside a beautifully appointed table and a row of chairs arranged to face a broad expanse of lawn.

Lady Alameda grinned at her. "Come along, dear. Don't tell me you wouldn't derive a certain satisfaction from whacking this little bluebird up into the air?" She dangled the cork whose feathers were precisely the shade of Lord St. Cleve's coat.

"You make a very good point." Elizabeth accepted the shuttlecock and a battledore from her.

Lady Alameda laughed. "Deli*th*ful!" She waved

her fan like a symphony conductor. "Listen carefully. I've made a few adjustments to the rules . . ."

Of course she had, Elizabeth expected nothing less from the enigmatic countess. Where normally it was played between a pair, Lady Alameda had cleverly adapted it for four players. Her servants had lain down two lines of potash in the grass, about five feet from each other. Down this alley one must not step, or a point would be lost.

Elizabeth gave the shuttlecock a gratifying thwack! It shot up, blue feathers quivering in the sunlight, and arced down directly at Miss Devious.

"Oh dear! Oh! Oh my." One would have thought a spider had crawled up the young woman's dress. She danced around, holding her battledore as if it were a wilting pancake. Anyone would have been certain the chit was going to miss. It surprised the stockings off Elizabeth when Miss Helpless gave it a hearty wallop and sent the thing soaring back up into the air.

"Bravo!" Robert applauded from the sidelines.

"Well done, Miss Dunworthy." St. Cleve all but shook his partner's hand. Miss Dunworthy beamed back at him ever so sweetly, a slight breeze waving her sprigged muslin endearingly around her legs.

Mr. Dunworthy declared his sister, "A brave little sport."

Lady Alameda chuckled.

The battledore hung limp in Elizabeth's hand, which was too bad, because the wretched shuttlecock was hurtling toward her.

"Look alive, Izzie!" Robert shouted.

Her partner, Lord Horton, gave her a tardy warning. "Above you, Lady Elizabeth. Above you."

She glanced up just in time to see cork and feathers nearly crack her in the forehead, and stumbled back trying to get out of the way. It landed in her lap.

Lord Horton rushed to her aid, supporting her shoulders. "Are you injured, my lady? Your ankle? Any other portion of your . . . Oh dear. I cannot think this is a proper entertainment for a lady of your refined nature." While he prattled on about how exceedingly delicate she was, while St. Cleve stood chuckling at her, and Miss Double-Devious had a smug little grin on her face. *The cat.*

Robert announced, "A point for Miss Dunworthy! Don't just sit there, Izzie. Get on with it."

Lord Horton protested. "I fear Lady Elizabeth has been incapacitated. Shall I carry you to a chair?"

"No, thank you. I am quite well. If you will simply help me up." The gown Lady Alameda had given her did not have nearly enough room in the skirt for an activity of this sort. Elizabeth got to her feet with as much dignity as possible. Shuttlecock in one hand and her weapon in the other, she prepared to do battle.

She smacked the cork, giving it very little arc, at St. Cleve, who still stood there chuckling at her like an overgrown jackanapes. It struck him in the chest. Elizabeth smiled innocently and fought back the urge to giggle at his surprised expression.

"Point for Izzie." Robert must have decided it was his duty to keep score.

She dusted grass particles from the back of her dress while St. Cleve batted the shuttlecock into the air. Play went to Lord Horton, who lined up for the shot, backed up, watched for the descent, but at the last minute shifted too far and ended up slightly off course. Luckily, he managed to lob it up to dear Miss Dunworthy, who handily whacked it to Elizabeth.

This time she was ready. She hit it early, cracking her paddle against the cork, sending it whirling crazily straight for St. Cleve's ear.

He waved the paddle at it, the way one swats at a mosquito buzzing by the ear. He managed to hit it, but it slammed with a puff into the potash line at his feet.

Mr. Dunworthy applauded Elizabeth. "Deadly shot!"

Robert hooted. "She caught you napping with that one, St. Cleve. Two points for Izzie."

His lordship didn't look too pleased as he bent to pick up the shuttlecock and dusted off its powdered feathers.

Elizabeth grinned at him and shrugged. "Beginners luck."

"I doubt it." He removed his coat and tossed it onto a chair by Lady Alameda. "Interesting game you've devised, Aunt Honore."

"Yes. I'm enjoying it thus far."

"The day is young."

"Just hit the thing."

He bowed. "With pleasure." He tossed up the shuttlecock, feinted as if hitting toward good old Pointy-Nose but instead he swerved and drove the bird to her. Elizabeth lunged for it and caught it with the edge of her battledore, flipping it into the air in a long predictable arc. But at least she'd hit it and won a "Well done!" from Lord Horton.

Unfortunately, Miss Devious used the distraction to land the hapless bluebird at Lord Horton's feet, which elicited a symphony of praise from her gloating partner and the sidelines. Elizabeth noted that the dear demure gel had quite forgotten to lisp as she accepted their praise. Extraordinary what the heat of battle will cure.

During the course of the game, Ruthless Miss Dunworthy discovered that a slapping shot aimed at Lord Horton's knees guaranteed her a point. No matter how he ran about the yard, jumping backward, or sliding sideways, he could not return the shuttlecock. After Miss Dunworthy's eighth point employing this tactic, Elizabeth could scarcely resist rushing to Horton's side of the grass and making the hit for him.

She glanced over and noticed his pallor. "Lord Horton? Are you well? Your face, it's quite red."

He wavered and pulled at his cravat. "The sun, I fear. A trifle warm."

"Perhaps you should remove your coat as Lord St. Cleve did. You are among friends." She scooped up the shuttlecock from the grass and held it out to him. He waved two fingers, declining. And she realized he was about to faint. His eyes rolled up and he collapsed into her arms.

Elizabeth stumbled backward trying to hold him up. St. Cleve rushed up beside her and tried to shift Horton's dead weight to him. But it was awkward, and in the end, Lord Horton slid down the front of her dress. Mr. Dunworthy, Robert, and Lord St. Cleve carried poor Lord Horton to the shade of a large tree where Lady Alameda had a tea table set out.

The countess presided over the medical ministrations. "He's scarcely breathing. Take that coat off him. And for pity's sake, remove that ridiculous cravat. His collar is so high, he probably strangled to death." She directed them with the authority of a general. "Unbutton his vest. Now the shirt. Tear it open, he's probably wearing a girdle. Yes, just as I thought. No wonder he overheated. Cut the laces, Valen. And stand back." The countess grabbed a pitcher full of lemon water and doused him. Lord Horton sputtered back to life, a lemon wedge resting atop the sparse hair of his chest.

The sight of poor Lord Horton in his undress quite overset Miss Dunworthy's delicate sensibilities. She started lisping incoherently. "I*th*'s horri*thy*ing. *Thi*mply *th*oo *th*oo much."

Robert chafed her fair hands and tried to soothe her. Lord St. Cleve suggested to Mr. Dunworthy that his sister might have experienced enough excitement for one day.

Revived, Lord Horton surveyed his lack of attire with nearly the same alarm as had Miss Dunworthy. His coat was gone, his cravat cast aside in the grass, his vest and shirt unbuttoned, and his girdle split open like a Sunday goose. He shook as he accepted the glass of water Lady Alameda offered. Gulping it down, he struggled to his feet, and attempted to button the top portion of his shirt, missing it by a row. One side puffed up higher than the other, testifying to an extraordinary amount of starch in it. The torn bottom half flapped out like a sail. Elizabeth concluded this would probably not be the day he kneeled at her feet and begged for her hand in marriage.

She couldn't honestly drum up much regret. Instead, relief pervaded her being, and genuine sympathy for poor hapless Pointy-Nose. He may be a dreadful poet, but he really was a gentle soul, a kind person.

Lord Horton gave up trying to do up his shirt and vest, glanced around completely flustered, and bowed to his hostess. "Thank you for your hospitality, Lady Alameda. A very pleasant afternoon. However, in light of . . . under these circumstances . . . I must take my leave. Lady Elizabeth, a delight, as always."

She handed him his coat. Lady Alameda extended his soiled cravat to him with two fingers as if the thing were contaminated. "Do come back again, Lord Horton. I'm all agag to hear more of your poetry."

Elizabeth murmured, "Agog. She means agog."

But Lord Horton didn't appear to be listening. He lurched unsteadily toward the house. Lady Alameda signaled and a footman hurried to assist the fleeing lord. Then she whirled around to her remaining guests. "Anyone care for tea and cakes?"

Elizabeth dropped into a chair, ready to devour a full glass of any sort of liquid and at least three cakes. But Lady Alameda pinched up her lips and shook her head disapprovingly. "Oh, my dear, just look at you." She waved her hand at the front of Elizabeth's dress.

Egad. Elizabeth dropped her head into her hand and massaged her forehead. The satin had absorbed every droplet of perspiration and formed stains. Rivulets had formed in some very embarrassing areas. She frowned skeptically at her hostess, who had pinched up her nose and was making a great show of her repulsion. The lady had known full well they would be playing battledore when she sent the clingy satin gown to Elizabeth.

Lady Alameda turned to her nephew. "Good heavens, Valen, you're dripping, too. The pair of you—exactly like a couple of racehorses. I daresay you must cool down properly. Take Lady Elizabeth for a walk; she is dreadfully overheated. Down by the trees where there is some shade." She fanned herself and turned to the others. "Oh, but Miss Dunworthy, how very clever you are not to sweat. You may stay at the table with us and have tea."

Lord St. Cleve held out his arm to Elizabeth. "Care for a trot around the park?"

Despite herself, she smiled at him and accepted his escort.

Valen glanced at her sideways. "You must forgive my aunt, she can be rather caustic at times. I'm certain she meant no insult, likening you to a race-horse. Probably meant it as a compliment."

"She likened you to a horse as well." Elizabeth smiled crookedly, and he noticed for the first time the delicate dimples that formed when she grinned. "I believe your aunt knows precisely what she is saying. Even so, I find it impossible to dislike her for it."

"You surprised me today, Lady Elizabeth. I thought you far more . . ." But then, he realized he had nowhere to go with the remark that would not insult her. He had thought her far too stuffy to play a game like Battledore, much less play it with such vigor. Neither could he forget the tale of her jumping off the roof.

"I'm well aware of what you think of me, my lord."

"Thought." Before he realized what he was doing, he found himself smoothing his hand over her elegant fingers resting on his sleeve. *Gad! I'm no better than Horton, petting her hands.* He let go and cleared his throat. "I would never have guessed you could play Battledore with such ferocity."

"Yes. And I would have won, too, if—"

"My lady, humility, humility." He pretended to scold her. "Do you really think I would have allowed you to trounce dear Miss Dunworthy? She would have been devastated. No. That would be completely unacceptable. Ungentlemanly."

"Allowed?" She yanked her hand away, stopped

walking and thrust both hands onto her hips. "I daresay, *dear Miss Dunworthy* can take care of herself. And what of you? You know perfectly well, you came within a hairsbreadth of losing."

"Losing? You cannot seriously think . . . Oh, but you do." He grinned at her. "I was merely humoring you."

Her mouth opened and closed in a series of little starts and gasps. "Humoring me?"

He shrugged. "Tossing you the odd point here and there. Setting a pitch you might hit to advantage. You were working excessively hard, even catching some of Horton's shots for him. A valiant effort. It was the least I could do."

Her lips clamped into a thin line as if holding back burgeoning flames she was readying to belch at him.

He decided to circumvent his execution. "You're reddening, Lady Elizabeth." He smiled seductively, fighting like mad not to laugh out loud. "You're supposed to be cooling down. It isn't good for a temperamental racehorse to overexcite herself." He took her hand and laid it on the crook of his arm, tugging her down the walk with him just as if she weren't about to explode.

Eventually, a puff of steam escaped her lips. "Oh, it's no use. You are utterly impossible."

"So I've been told."

A thrush swooped across their path and glided to safety in the trees. "Apparently, you haven't always been a docile little lamb either."

"My wretched brother." She shook her head and muttered, "He ought not to have told that flying story."

"Not the ordinary thing one expects from a little girl."

"Hmm. Yes. I believe my father mentioned that point, one or two times."

Valen saw it again, the hurt he'd noticed earlier. "He didn't actually take a horsewhip to you, did he?"

"I don't see that it matters." Her lovely nose tilted up an inch or two.

"Did he?"

"A willow branch."

Valen swore.

"Heavens. You needn't curse. It isn't as if I didn't deserve it. The roof was three stories high. Robert could have been killed. It was reckless in the extreme. Foolhardy."

Reckless. Foolish. The very words Valen had heard rehearsed into his ears all his life. He took a deep breath and stared blindly out at the edge of the park. "Nevertheless, I cannot like the man for doing it." His fingers found hers again. "I'm glad he didn't beat out all of your spirit."

She said nothing for a moment. A clump of purple lupine leaned its heavy head over the edge of the pathway. Bees whisked in and out among the flowers. Izzie leaned down to catch the scent of a lily peeking out from the shade. "Ironic isn't it, that my father should have expected me to be so tame. During his life, he took such daring risks."

Valen frowned. "You speak of him as if he were dead? Robert told me he was in America trying to salvage what's left of his investments."

She attempted a wry chuckle, but it failed to convince him that she was cavalier on the subject. "Robert is ever the optimist. I suspect Papa drowned at sea, or worse. We haven't heard from him for over two years. Our older brother sailed out last August in search of him. We've had no word from him either."

"Ships are often commandeered in the Atlantic.

The mail abandoned. I suppose, it is possible, a letter might be lost for years." It sounded hollow. Still, wasn't some hope better than none? "Or a brother," he added quietly.

"So I've heard." She smiled patiently at him, clearly unconvinced. "Mother has nearly gone mad with worry. She's taken to dosing herself with patent medicines to calm her nerves. I tried to dissuade her—prepared some herbs to ease her tension. But I'm afraid she would rather sit in a stupor."

"And so you concocted this plan to marry in order to repair the family coffers."

"It seemed a sensible thing to do."

It was logical. Other families had adopted the exact same measures. And yet, he couldn't keep the disapproving tone out of his voice. "Perhaps."

Lady Elizabeth didn't seem to notice. "St. Cleve is a lesser title, is it not? Tied to a small estate, probably? An allowance of a thousand or two a year, I should think?" She turned to him as if merely posing an innocent question.

Does she honestly think I do not notice her calculating in my direction?

"Hmm. Yes. Something along those lines."

She glanced into the trees and sighed, and she may as well have said aloud, "What a pity."

Her disappointment was not entirely displeasing. Valen smiled. He decided to toy with her. "Not nearly enough, is it? Naturally, that lets me off your list of eligibles."

"Don't be crass." Ah, there was the familiar sour pucker he'd come to enjoy so well.

"Not crass, my lady. Frank. If you are worried about my feelings, allow me to reassure you. I'm not wounded in the least. To the contrary, I'm heartily relieved to know it."

"How very fortunate." She glared at him, tapping her toe against the stones of the pathway. "I do, however, find it odd, considering *I* am not the one who went about kissing people in the middle of the night, making them speculate on such matters."

So, she *had* speculated on it. Good. He'd lain awake for an abominably long time, enduring scenario after scenario of tortuously pleasant imaginings. She deserved to share in his sleeplessness. "Yes, it's a great comfort knowing I will be spared any of your machinations."

She stamped her foot on the pathway and turned to him, ready to bite. "Machinations! Me? I do not machinate anyone!"

"I'm not certain that's proper usage of the word." He pretended to cogitate on her grammar for a moment before bearing down on her, pressing forward, so that she had to look up at him. "But I have observed you closely, my dear, and you *do* machinate. Poor Horton has no idea which way is up. You have convinced him to sup quite eagerly out of your slipper. And I ask you, *Lord Horton?* Could you not pick a fellow with more backbone? Someone a trifle more worthy of your—"

"*He* has thirty thousand a year." She said it as if it were a slap to his face.

"Does he? A very convincing argument. I wish you happy."

"Oh? And what of you and Miss Devious-Dunworthy? Do you think your paragon of feminine virtues isn't hanging out for a title? Then you are more fool than I thought. Yet, I doubt you will accuse her of *machinations.*"

"You can't be jealous?"

"Don't be tedious." She stepped back and crossed her arms.

"I am never tedious."

She thrust her finger at him. "You are. You are tedious this very minute."

He grabbed the accusatory finger, and clasped her hand in his, like a fluttering bird in his palm. She stared at her captive hand. The pulse quickened in her neck.

He spoke softly, issuing a challenge. "You might not think me so tedious, if I were to kiss you again." It was a fool thing to say. He didn't care.

She appeared properly alarmed. Yet, she didn't try to wrench free. Her hand quivered in his palm. He felt her heart beating wildly.

Valen had an insane urge to laugh, run, pull her along beside him. Instead, he decided to irritate her. "After all, it caused you to *speculate* last night."

She drew back, her breast swelling indignantly. She was so *confounded* appealing. Suddenly, he realized the wild heartbeat in his hand might be his own. *Dangerous*. Still, he couldn't let go. "It would seem kissing you is the only way to escape your haranguing tongue."

She arched her brow. "Oh? We're discussing my tongue again, are we?" They stood far too close.

He swallowed. His voice caught on something low in his throat. He was in trouble. "See. You're doing it this very minute." He let go of her hand and stepped back. "Machinating me. Well, it won't work. I see right through you."

And so he did. Her gown clung to her in remarkably descriptive ways. He shook his head, half grinning. "You are a diabolically clever woman. I don't know how you do it, but I'm not going to succumb. No, my lady, I won't kiss you. No matter how much you beguile me." His treacherous feet carried him back to her, close enough to reach down and . . .

Her chin tilted up. Was it an invitation, or her damnable pride?

"Nothing could be further from my mind." Her pretty nose sniffed with disdain. "In fact, I will slap you soundly should you even attempt such a thing. And, I am certainly *not* beguiling you."

But, she was beguiling him. The pinkness climbing her neck, the flutter of her hand to her breast, the pout on her lips, the wistful flicker in her eyes. *All—maddeningly alluring.*

In about two seconds, he would haul her into the trees and give her a good sound kissing, a kissing she well and truly deserved. His conscience spoke firmly, reining in his rash thoughts, scolding him for falling so neatly into her feminine gambit.

He shook his head and allowed himself to laugh aloud. "Enough. I cry craven." He smiled at her, raising his hands in defeat. "You win." Valen wasn't sure what game they'd been playing at, but she'd just stolen all the points.

Odd. She ought to look triumphant, rather than so enticingly disappointed. He had that urge again, to pull her into the trees and . . . "Perhaps we ought to return to the others."

Her brow pinched up. She nodded her agreement and in stern tones added, "Splendid idea."

Valen could not help but note the small sigh that escaped her lips as they turned around on the path, a tiny thing—almost imperceptible. It pleased him. In all probability it was just another of her machinations. Even so, he liked it.

Chapter 8

'Tis Better to Weave Than to Rip

While Robert paced in the entry hall, Valen leaned in the doorway of his aunt's study with a brandy in his hand. He hadn't seen Izzie since the previous afternoon. She'd been cloistered away in her rooms, and he'd been busy at his tailors, fitting the new green peacock coat. Vain fowl everywhere would soon squawk with jealousy. The coat was sufficiently grotesque to draw everyone's attention at Lady Ashburton's ball.

Robert dropped into a chair next to the study door. "Come with us, Valen. Dead bore these balls. Don't know if I can tolerate it on my own."

"Courage man. I'll be along later. Promised my aunt I'd accompany her. She prefers to straggle in after everyone else has arrived. Insists on making an impressive entrance."

"Wish I was going late. Can't abide all that standing in line, and how-do-you-do nonsense. And then there's dinner. Stuck listening to a sour old baroness on one hand, and some horse-face chit prattling on t'other."

"Perhaps you will be lucky enough to entertain Miss Dunworthy on one side."

Robert sat up. "Capital thought. Do you really think she might be there?"

"I have it on good authority. I promised to be her partner for one of the sets."

Robert's face brightened. "Excellent news. Tell you what. If you don't arrive in time, I shall be happy to fulfill your obligation."

Valen swirled his brandy. "Noble of you."

"Least I can do." Robert slapped his hands on his thighs and stood up. "Where is that sister of mine? Long past time we were leaving."

Izzie, as if on cue, appeared on the stairs. Valen nearly let his glass slip out of his fingers. He caught it and took a good stiff swallow, scarcely noticing the sharp fruity bite of the liquor. *How had she done it?* She'd paired that bold peacock fabric with a white fairylike underdress and the effect was . . . He realized his mouth was hanging open as if he were a blasted schoolboy. He couldn't help it. Neither could he take his eyes off her.

Robert hurried forward. "There you are. Thought you wanted to get there before supper. Been waiting upwards to a half hour."

Her chin went up. Black curls draped down one side of her neck, dancing enticingly against the pale curve of her breast. "I did my best."

Robert stepped back. "Never mind. You do look rather well tonight, Izzie. Don't you think so, Valen?"

Valen pulled his jaw together and swallowed, suddenly unable to look at her. He nodded. "Very well." He finished the contents of his glass. *Very well, indeed.*

He escaped into the study and shut the door. She looked like an angel, a sweet, innocent, very desirable angel. And he was about to make people laugh at her.

Valen stood at the window staring out at the blackness of the night. He strained to see a handful of stars glittering through the London haze, or glimpse the shadow of trees at the edge of the park. What he couldn't escape, and saw all too readily, was his own reflection in the glass. It didn't please him.

What had he become, that he would humiliate a young woman this way? He hated her arrogance. Hated all of the beau monde for their self-important airs, the way they treated with contempt anyone who didn't have a suitable wardrobe or a significant enough pedigree to warrant their approval. He despised pompous aristocrats like his grandfather, who had treated Valen's mother as if she were nothing more than dross. *May he rot in hell.* They deserved to be ridiculed, mocked, taught a lesson.

But did Izzie? That was the question.

He turned away from the window and refilled his brandy snifter. She'd worked so hard on that blasted gown. It was brilliant. "Although"—he raised his glass arguing his case to the dim room—"it really ought to conceal more of her . . . her charms." He couldn't stop picturing exactly which charms it ought to conceal. He knew full well other men would not be able to resist looking at her either.

He concocted a scenario wherein he wore the hideous peacock coat to Lady Ashburton's. Izzie would hurry out of the ballroom. Safe from leering eyes. Valen would run after her, and offer to bring her home, just the two of them in the carriage, and . . . He shook off the ridiculous daydream. In truth, the high and mighty Lady Elizabeth would never forgive him. She would, in all likelihood, ring a peal over his head loud enough to put the bells of St. Paul to shame. *Furthermore, I'd deserve it.*

If he wore the coat, he'd be tormenting her. Not so different from his grandfather, after all. He suddenly had no desire to attend Lady Ashburton's ball.

The study door opened. "What's this? Brooding?" Honore gave him her usual thrust to the throat.

He set his glass on the desk and refused to parry.

"Well?" She bent over an oil lamp and lit it. "Obviously you aren't going over the household accounts. What can be plaguing you?" She tapped her cheek. "Hmm. Let me guess? Could it be someone who carries her nose rather high in the air?"

"Taken up mind reading, have you?"

"Good grief, Valen. Don't need a crystal ball to read you. Now, go put on something hideous, and we shall go see what trouble we can churn up at Lady Ashburton's." His aunt looked positively eager.

He sighed. "Don't know if I have anything suitably revolting."

"How very odd. Just this afternoon, one of the maids told me she came across a ghastly green and orange coat in your rooms. A coat so revolting it would make the *Beau* cross his eyes and faint dead away."

He folded his arms and frowned at her. It shouldn't come as any surprise that she spied on him.

"Oh, don't get all up in the boughs. Put the ugly thing on and let us be on our way."

"I find it no longer fits."

"Whatever do you pay your tailor for, my dear boy? You just brought it home today." When he didn't answer, she continued, "Fortunately, I have just the thing, one of my stepsons, Marcus's, coats. Perhaps not as garish as you prefer, but a trifle too green for my taste."

Valen tilted his head, trying to decipher his aunt's motives. She was up to something. He had little doubt of it. She smiled, innocent as a lamb, albeit a very crafty lamb. Or, more likely, a cantankerous she-goat preparing to butt some unsuspecting passerby in the hindquarters. How could he resist such a game?

"Very well. Let's have a look at this coat."

Chapter 9

Stick a Pin in It

Lady Elizabeth stood in Lady Ashburton's magnificent ballroom, the walls covered in watered gold satin and large ornate mirrors. She stared bleakly at her three suitors, Lord Looks-Like-A-Cherub, Sir Blah, and Lord Horton of the Pointy-Nose. Instead of comparing their bank accounts, she found herself entertaining the troublesome question of which one had the most backbone. If only she hadn't cut St. Cleve's rant short, she might have heard the end of his sentence. "Someone more worthy of—" *Of what?* What was it he thought her suitor should be more worthy of? It gnawed at her. Annoying her all the more because she couldn't keep from glancing toward the enormous double doors, hoping to see a tall man enter, his gold-red hair tied back as if he'd newly arrived from the Georgian age, and wearing a perfectly dreadful ensemble.

Lord Horton interrupted her thoughts. "My Lady, is there something troubling you? If you don't care to perform the waltz with me, I will withdraw my offer."

St. Cleve isn't even present and I'm frowning. Drat him. He will have me wrinkled up like an old crone inside of a fortnight. She smoothed out her brow. "Oh, dear me, no. I would adore waltzing with you. I'm simply concerned that I may not know the steps as well as I ought. I shall have to depend upon you to guide me."

He puffed up, smiling warmly. "Never fear. I will be happy to teach you."

Sir Blah muttered, "I'll just wager you will."

Lord Looks-Like–A-Cherub chuckled. "Daresay, it wants a fellow what can move without the confinement of a harness." He and Sir Blah must have thought this comment enormously funny for they nearly fell upon one another in their hysterics.

Lord Horton turned pink. Elizabeth surmised the story of his collapse at Lady Alameda's had made the rounds. Now who, she wondered, could have distributed the tale? A quick glance at Miss Devious-Dunworthy giggling with Robert and two other couples answered the question. Her brother would think it a great lark, and Miss Devious would find it a useful attention-getting tale.

Elizabeth took a deep breath. "I trust you completely, my lord. I'm honored you would undertake the task." She inclined her head graciously. "Indeed, I cannot think of anyone I would rather have instruct me." She laced her remark with a hint of seduction. Enough seduction that Sir Blah and Lord Looks-Like–A-Cherub stopped laughing abruptly.

Lord Cherubic protested and tried to recover his advantage. "Oh no. That is to say, I mean, dash it all, Lady Elizabeth. If you're serious about learning the steps, I'd be happy to escort you to the balcony where we might practice in private."

The others glared at him as if he were completely balmy for making such an improper suggestion.

"Didn't mean it like that. Good heavens, it isn't as if we'd be in the dark. Lady Ashburton has enough torches out there to light half of London. A bit of privacy, that's all, to learn the steps without everyone watching."

Sir Blah frowned skeptically.

Lord Horton regained his confidence. "Hardly necessary, old boy. I can manage the lesson right here in *public*." He emphasized the "ck" sound on the end of public, sending Lord Looks-Like–A-Cherub into the sulks. Apparently, her handsome suitor didn't have the requisite backbone, either.

She turned to Sir Blah, appraising the condition of his spine for a moment, and then sighed. At least he had twenty thousand a year. Perhaps she should give him a chance. According to rumor, he didn't gamble, didn't drink overmuch, and his only excess was spending a substantial amount of time and money on an enormous pack of hunting dogs. She smiled at Sir Blah and could almost hear a lifetime of yipping in the background.

Fortunately, the noise proved to be the musicians, merely warming up for the promenade to the waltz. Lord Horton placed her hand on his arm. They started their march around the perimeter of the room and he showed her how to point her toe. She knew perfectly well how to do it, but it pleased him to play teacher.

At that moment, a hubbub at the entrance signaled the arrival of latecomers. A footman announced the Countess de Alameda and her nephew, Lord St. Cleve.

Elizabeth's hand flew to clamp her stupid heart in place. The wretched thing seemed to have forgotten its rhythm. When she got a proper look at him, it did nothing to calm her idiot pulse. Her hands tensed. She developed a problem breathing too rapidly. The scoundrel had on a green coat, the color being an almost identical match to the green of her gown.

"Are you quite well, my dear?" Horton chafed her rigid hand.

No. She was not well. She was angry enough to stab pins into a certain overgrown green coat. *Behave like a lady.* She gritted her teeth and mustered a weak smile. "I am well, thank you. May I say, Lord Horton, you are extraordinarily considerate. The very image of a gentleman." *Unlike some men in my acquaintance, backbone or not.*

Elizabeth and Lord Horton paraded nearly halfway around the ballroom, when a formidable trio impeded their progress. Like the prow of a large ship ramming a pier, Lady Bessborough and her imposing bosom blocked their path. Beside her, stood Lady Alameda, and their hostess, Lady Ashburton.

A long violet ostrich feather drooped over Lady Bessborough's mountainous coiffure. "What's this I hear, young Horton? Naughty poems?"

The color washed out of his cheeks. Elizabeth feared he might faint again.

"Delightfully wicked poems. Tell her all about them, Horty." Lady Alameda nodded enthusiastically, giving him no time to speak. "Brilliant use of erotic symbolism. Subtle. Very *feathery*." Her eyebrows waggled suggestively. "I nearly swooned the first time I heard him. Truly remarkable. Wait till you hear the part about a ladybird climbing upon his soaring wing."

"Why Horton, you slyboots! Didn't know you had it in you." Lady Bessborough laughed loudly, and slapped him on the shoulder. "Something of your father's disposition after all."

Horton's color seemed to return after that last dubitable compliment, but he remained too astonished to speak.

"We wish to hear these ditties." After using the royal "*we*," Lady Bessborough looped her arm through his dangling limb and tugged him out to sea.

Lady Ashburton glanced around, both excited and anxious, and whispered behind her fan to Lady Alameda. "Oh dear. How erotic are these poems?"

Lady Alameda, who was busy maneuvering herself in between Elizabeth and Lord Horton, took hold of his other arm. "Well, my dear, I can tell you this. I had to dismiss him from my sitting room. There were young ladies present." She glanced pointedly at Elizabeth. "I feared they might get over excited."

Lady Ashburton tittered. "I'm all agog."

"My sentiments exactly." Lady Alameda and her cohorts ushered the unwitting poet away.

He cast a pleading backward glance at Elizabeth. "But I . . . I promised Lady Elizabeth . . ."

"Oh, never mind that. My nephew offered to take your place. He'll be along to collect her shortly."

"But I would rather, that is to say, my poems are not—" Pointy-Nose made a feeble attempt to resist his captors.

"Now Horton, look lively!" Lady Alameda ordered. "We've gathered a very distinguished audience in Lady Ashburton's drawing room to hear these bawdy poems of yours."

Lady Ashburton patted her palms together eagerly, but with the soft fabric of her gloves it made almost no sound. "Oh yes! You will be all the talk, Lord Horton. All the talk. Lord Byron move over, I say. Nothing like a good arousing poem."

"Amelia!" Lady Bessborough rebuked her friend loud enough for half the occupants of the room to hear. "You're flushed already. Do try to control yourself, my dear."

Elizabeth stood dumbfounded as they dragged away Lord Horton and his Missing Spine to begin a career as an erotic poet. She stepped out of the promenade pathway. Her hand fluttered up helplessly in a half wave of farewell.

Someone captured her floating hand and bowed over it, someone in a green coat. "May I?"

By the time she composed herself enough to skewer Lord St. Cleve properly, it was too late. The waltz had begun and he held her in his arms, his green-sleeved arms.

As St. Cleve whirled her into step beside the other waltzing couples, she caught sight of Sir Blah and Lord Not-So-Cherubic nudging one another and falling in line behind the matrons and their naughty poet. A veritable parade of guests streamed out of the ballroom after them. "Well, that's that then," she muttered and glanced up at Lord St. Cleve.

He was studying her. "Are you disappointed?"

The question caught her off guard. Too late to hide the play of emotions that must surely be marching across her face. If only he would look away. *Disappointed?* To have exchanged pasty Lord Horton and his girdle for Lord St. Cleve, whose hand on her back guided her with strength and confidence, whose sprinkling of mischievous freckles belied the intensity of his eyes and the firm line of his jaw? *Hardly*.

Yet, she could not forget, he had only a few thousand a year compared to Lord Horton's thirty. There was also the matter of the coat. Not to mention his abominable lack of fashion sense, and a dozen other annoying habits. "I don't know how to answer that."

He almost smiled at her. "Ah, my dear, your honesty astonishes me."

One of his dozen or so annoying habits was the uncanny ability to lace his comments with barbs. She sniffed at him. "Are you trying to flatter me?"

His wicked dimples curled into existence. "You don't need flattery, my lady." He smiled as he glanced away, guiding them through a turn.

"And what precisely does that mean?"

"Haven't you enough flatterers in your court?"

"No."

He tilted his head, chiding her with a single look. "Tut tut, Izzie. Honesty."

"Don't tut-tut me. You are not my father. Nor my governess. And you may address me as Lady Elizabeth."

His impudent grin ought to have faded, but it stayed securely in place. "You're frowning, my dear. Mustn't pucker your brow in public. People will think I'm torturing you rather than waltzing."

"They would be correct. While we're on the subject of torture, I wish you will stop persecuting me in this childish manner."

"Persecuting?"

"Trying to embarrass me. Your coat." She glanced at the sidelines. Two debutantes in white

ruffled gowns nodded in their direction and tittered. "You see. People are laughing at us."

"You have a vivid imagination. I doubt anyone is
laughing at us. Who would care about such a triv-
ial matter?"

"They are. I saw them laughing."

"Nonsense. The whole world does not set their
clocks by you."

"I'm well aware of that."

"Good. Then don't wrinkle up your brow so fe-
rociously or they will be snickering at your prune
face instead of the color of our clothing."

Prune face, indeed! And it will be all his fault. "This
is the third time, is it not, that we have matched? I
do not believe for one instant that it is simply a coincidence your coat is the exact color of my dress.
You did it on purpose."

"I assure you, Lady Elizabeth. It is precisely that,
a coincidence. More to the point, we don't match.
There is not one peacock on this coat. While you
have a veritable flock of them on your gown."

"Splitting hairs. It's as if you snuck into my
room, saw from a distance the fabric I was sewing
and copied it. These peacocks blend with the
background color to form the very shade of green
you are wearing."

"Sewing? And here I thought you were merely
reading late at night."

"So you did spy on me."

"You wound me, my lady. Were I to spy on you, I
would do a far better job of it. I would find the
exact fabric and produce a coat far more interesting than this dull old thing. This happens to be my
cousin's coat. I borrowed it for the evening. My
coat was . . ." His dimples disappeared and he
swung her forcefully into the half turn, narrowly

avoiding another couple. ". . . no longer suit-able."

She stared at him. He was earnest. His coat certainly didn't resemble the horrid creation with huge lapels he'd worn to Lady Sefton's breakfast. No, this one fit his broad shoulders perfectly and hung as if Weston himself had designed it. *Perplexing*.

He leaned in, speaking nearer to her ear. "Further to the point, if I were to sneak into your room late at night, let me assure you, it would certainly *not* be for a look at your fabric."

Elizabeth blinked. She felt the jostle of his shoulder under her hand. He was chuckling at her. He'd just made a lurid remark, hadn't he? *Yes. Yes, he had*. She felt a rush of heat prickle up her neck. "I ought to slap you for that remark."

"Should you? Why?"

"It was unseemly."

"Oh, well, in that case, slap away, my dear. But first, tell me, what must I do to you for wearing that unseemly gown?"

"My gown?" She glanced down to see if something had fallen off or ripped open or . . . Her brow pinched together again. "It is perfectly respectable."

"It is not."

They were in the middle of a turn, so she glanced over her shoulder checking in one of Lady Ashburton's huge gilded mirrors to see if there was something wrong with the back of her gown. "You are gammoning me."

"I never gammon."

"Ha! There's a tale. Where is this honesty you prize so highly? Nothing is wrong with my gown."

"A very clever construction. I'll grant you that. But I figured it out, and it is unseemly. You made it look as if the real dress is falling away and you are left in nothing but your wispy underclothes."

She gasped and pulled her hand from his shoulder to cover her breast. "How can you say such a thing?"

"Honesty." He grinned. "And yes, it's too low there, too."

How had he deduced the precise mechanism of her design so easily? Confusing man. What was he? Like his hair, gold one minute, strawberry the next. A frilled fop with a physique any Corinthian would envy. All she could do for a moment was breathe and let him whirl her around the room. He looked so smug, so sure of himself, so irritatingly in control. Well, no more.

Elizabeth returned her hand to his shoulder and relaxed in his arms. On the next turn, she pretended to have difficulty maneuvering and allowed herself to float just a trifle too close to him. There it was. That flicker of uncertainty in his eyes. She smiled softly and turned her head as if completely disinterested. His arms stiffened and she felt a delicious sense of triumph. When she brushed ever so slightly against the inside of his muscular thigh he nearly stumbled. Balance had been restored to her universe. Just in the nick of time, too, for the ending strains of the waltz sounded.

She took particular delight in the confused expression on Lord St. Cleve's face as he led her off the floor and over to her brother and Miss Dunworthy. Elizabeth decided to needle him. "Are you ill, my lord? You look a bit unsettled? A gastric disturbance, perhaps?"

It startled her when one of his dimples made an unexpected appearance. She'd thought she'd imprisoned them for the rest of the evening. But no, there it was, quirking evilly up on one side.

"This is far from over, Izzie," he whispered, bowing over her hand.

Instead of letting go, he pressed his lips against her lace-gloved fingers. No quick kiss. St. Cleve pressed on her a scandalous, overly warm thing that sent outlandish sensations up her arm and made her cheeks hot.

Elizabeth may have been the only one who gasped, but she felt as if everyone in the room must be holding their breath, everyone must be watching him linger over her hand too long, everyone observing the evocative lift of his brow. She stood there like a fish knocked on the head, utterly stunned. He laughed. Or was that Miss Dunworthy chuckling?

St. Cleve turned away and left her standing there like a marooned mackerel as he escorted Miss I-Despise-Her-Dunworthy out onto the ballroom floor. Elizabeth could still feel his lips on her hand. As her arm hung limp at her side, she gently twitched her fingers. The sensation remained. *Drat him.*

Chapter 10

Green Sleeves

"I hate men. They are all wretches!"

Late that night, long after Lord Horton discovered he did, indeed, have a gift for subtle erotic verse, and after the interminable carriage ride home, wherein Elizabeth was subjected to her brother rhapsodizing over the unparalleled beauty and exquisite charm of Miss Dunworthy, Elizabeth sat brooding on her bed.

"I hate them all." It was true, too. Honestly. Even her father, who never should have abandoned them. She hated him for it. Thoughtless. Typical man. You can't depend on them. How could he do it? He'd been her rudder. Her anchor. And now she was adrift in an ocean of confusion without him. Their entire family was in danger of sinking. How was she supposed to manage it all without him?

Perhaps, she didn't hate Robert, not altogether. How could she? But sometimes it seemed as if he had nothing but pigweed for brains. And Lord Horton appeared to be little more than a spineless twit. Unreliable. Why couldn't he be intelligent, capable and manly . . . but no, he wasn't. She hated them. Most of all, she hated Lord St. Cleve. Truly.

The reasons were unclear. He made her feel petty and feeble. He questioned the purity of her motives, called her dishonest, and accused her of machinating. However, none of those pierced the heart of the matter. No. The true reason escaped her, slipped around, sliding at the edge of her mind, just beyond her grasp.

She flopped back against the pillows, too tired to sort it out tonight. The oil lamp flickered and needed to be turned out. She slid off the bed. As she did, she heard scratching at the door.

She carried the lamp with her and whispered, "Who is it?"

"Lord St. Cleve's servant, mum."

"Not you again," she muttered. "Go away."

"I come bearing gifts."

She unlocked the door, a precaution she'd considered prudent in light of St. Cleve's vulgar comments at the ball, and peeped out. "What is it?"

"A package, Miss. His lordship says I'm required to deliver it with a poem, seeing as how the lady is fond of poetry."

St. Cleve's manservant, the same unkempt fellow who looked better suited to a post as a prison guard than a servant, stood in the hallway holding a package wrapped in brown paper and string. One of his stockings hung at his ankle; he was too plump for his jacket and one of the buttons was missing. "You need a new livery."

"Just what I mentioned to His Grace. But he says, 'Fine feathers do not a cockerel make.' "

"He's not a duke."

"No."

"Then, you ought not address him as 'Your Grace.' "

"No, mum. An' so I says to His Highness, not much of a cock without flash feathers, is he?"

Elizabeth sighed. "Just so. Now, if you will kindly deliver your package, I was preparing to take a short nap before the sun comes up."

"Aye, and here it is." He hefted the package but did not hand it to her. "An' this is the poem. He made me practice till I had it perfect. Says to apologize to you because it isn't smutty enough, but he will leave that sort of thing to a fellow, w' the name of Horton or Hortense." He scratched at his wig.

"Do get on with it."

"Yes, mum." He pulled at the skin on his throat and coughed lightly as if that might aid his recital.

"Sometime this age, if you please."

He stretched out his arm, mimicking a great stage actor.

> *Here is a gift for you, my sweet,*
> *Perchance to see what might have been*
> *And speculate on what might yet be;*
> *Ponder the raiment of lilies, dear:*
> *What will they wear when next we meet?*

He lowered his arm as if it were over.

"Go on. Where's the rest of it?"

"That's it."

"Hardly a poem, is it? An abysmal ditty, at best. He required you memorize *that* in the middle of the night?" She shook her head. "You have my sympathy. He might just as well have written it on a scrap of paper and told you to toss it at me."

"Oh, I don't know, miss. It's as fine a poem as any, I expect. Rhymes, true enough, don't it. Sweet. Meet. Dear and wear. P'rhaps not exact, but it sounds—"

"Thank you." Elizabeth had had enough of St. Cleve's inept servant and pathetic poetry. She seized the bundle from him and pushed the door shut with her foot. Carrying the gift to her bed, she set down the lamp, untied the knot, folded back the paper and unfurled the contents. There, on her bed, lay the most horrid coat in all of creation. A coat made out of the exact fabric of her gown. She held it up to the light.

"Good heavens. I must say, he was right. It is a great deal more interesting than the dull thing he wore tonight." Elizabeth ran her fingertips over the orange satin collar. The preposterous coat would have made a mockery of her dress. She would have been the laughingstock of the ball, of the season. Teased for months. Why hadn't he worn it?

The ridiculous thing smelled vaguely of him. Pressing the collar to her nose, she recognized the smell of his shaving soap and that other scent, the musky male scent that spoke only of him. Elizabeth slid her arms into the sleeves and smiled at the way they hung down past her fingers.

What had he said in the poem? Something about lilies, my sweet, when next we meet. She ran to the door and threw it open. Where had that idiot servant gotten to? She had to hear that poem one more time. Had it been a warning, or a promise?

The hall stretched empty and dark in both directions. The marble floor felt cool on her bare feet as she tiptoed away from her room. Thinking she heard the rustle of movement, she turned and whispered, "St. Cleve?" But there was only stillness in response. Silly that she should call his name. Sillier still that she should think he might appear in her hallway in the middle of the night. Even more absurd, the dreadful sinking sensation in the pit of her stomach when he did not.

She murmured his name one more time and reluctantly turned back to her room. Her mind was playing tricks on her now. She thought she glimpsed his shadow at the end of the hall. Imagined him reaching for her. She must be delirious for want of sleep. His poem had sounded more like a warning, a threat, than . . . than what? What had she hoped it might be? *Foolish. Ladies do not lose their heads nor their hearts.* She shut her door and leaned against it, listening for the sound of his footsteps. Unsure of what she would do if she heard them.

The remainder of the night, Valen twisted and yanked on his bedcovers, mauling them into tangled disarray during a dismal attempt to sleep. He kept hearing Elizabeth call him, whisper his name. But, of course, that was ridiculous. She held him in contempt. Typical behavior of her inbred aristocratic species. Gad, how grateful he was for having a commoner for a mother. He couldn't stomach the *ton* and their haughty ways. A wagonload of pampered milksops, the lot of them. It was nearly choking the life out of him to play their game. He put his pillow over his head to drown out the sound of her voice calling him.

"Lord St. Cleve? Capt'n? Wake up, sir. You gave me orders, sir. I was to wake you. Now, have pity on me and wake up, Captain."

"Sergeant Biggs, if that is you, I will have you drawn and quartered."

"Very well, Captain, but I was doing no more'n my duty. Following your orders, sir. The young lady received a note. She left the house not five minutes ago."

Valen tossed the pillow to the end of the bed and sat up. "What note? From who?"

"Well, it weren't from the Queen Mother, I can tell you that. Written on plain paper, and whoever it was, only give the maid a ha'penny to deliver it to the lady."

Valen swung his legs over the edge of the bed. "And you're just telling me about it now? Devil take it, man. Where are my boots?"

"I expect you'll be needing a good deal more than that. The watch might be alert to a fellow wearing nothing save his boots." He handed him a stack of clothing.

"For pity's sake. Don't stand there jawing me to death. Get the rest of my gear."

Biggs hurried to the wardrobe. "Just making a point, sir. P'rhaps you ought to wear a nightshirt to bed, like a proper gentleman."

"London is corrupting you, Biggs. A proper gentleman may wear whatever the hell he wants. What time is it, anyway?"

"Eight of the clock, your honor."

"What can she be doing at this hour?" Valen pulled on his trousers.

"I've no notion. Will you be requiring the short sword, my lord?"

"Most assuredly. And the pistol, I think."

"Pistol. Right you are. Will you be wanting me to come along then?"

Valen buttoned the top of his cambric shirt and slid into the long coat Biggs held out for him. "If you weren't gadded up like a butterfly in that blasted livery, I would. But no, you'll slow me down if I have to wait."

Biggs' shoulders slumped slightly.

"Next time, man. Now, tell me, did you observe her direction?"

"O' course, I did. Watched her from the window." Biggs followed him down the stairs, relating everything he'd seen.

Valen rubbed at his unshaven chin. He had a fair notion where Lady Elizabeth might be headed.

Chapter 11

Smashed Strawberries and Buttercup Silk

Elizabeth hurried down Water Street. Early in the morning, the street bore nothing of the pleasant bustle it would acquire later in the day. There were several occupants, but they trudged dourly about their business scarcely exchanging a nod. She pressed the handle and entered the shop. "Mr. Smythe?"

The curtain dividing the room stirred. Mr. Smythe pushed it aside. "You've come, at last. This way, my lady." He waved her into the back room. "He's here, and none too happy for the wait." Mr. Smythe hurried to the door she'd just entered and threw the bolt, locking it. "Quickly. We must be discreet."

"I should be more comfortable out here at the counter."

"He won't like it. Has all the prime goods in the back room. Spread out on a table like a veritable feast. I told him you were a lady. So, he's done it up proper. But he don't have all day. Getting an itchy foot this very minute."

"Very well." She ducked hesitantly under the curtain into the dimly lit warehouse area. There was, indeed, a grand display of silks spread on a long table. Beside the colorful array of fabrics stood a gentleman clad in an elegant black coat. She knew in a trice, simply by the cut of his coat and his bearing, the cloth would all be too expensive. Still, perhaps, she might bargain with him. Elizabeth could not resist fingering a soft, nearly translucent, peach sarcenet. It felt as if it had been woven from a cloud. "Divine."

He inclined his head to her. "You have excellent taste, Lady Elizabeth."

She detected the faintest hint of a French accent, expertly disguised. An Englishman might affect a French accent, but he would not then strive to hide it. "And you are?"

"A simple merchant, at your service." He bowed without any of the self-consciousness of a tradesman.

"Hmm." She turned over the corner of a cream and purple paisley, so deftly woven that she could find no trace of the warp threads. "This is exquisite. So exquisite, in fact, that I am certain your wares are beyond my touch." She turned to go.

"Before you leave, my lady, allow me, if you please, to show you a very special silk. It is as if it were made expressly for you."

She hesitated. What would it hurt to look? On the other hand, it might hurt a great deal. She'd already seen two pieces of cloth she would not easily forget. Her lack of funds made it all quite impossible. "I am very sorry. Mr. Smythe promised me something unique. I had no idea he would find such fine quality silks. These are not mere fabrics. They are works of art. You deserve far more than I can give for them." She brushed the curtain aside and hurried out.

Mr. Smythe rushed after her. "Lady Elizabeth, wait. Can you not, at least, look at the silk he selected for you? A man of such superior discrimination. Are you not curious?"

His words brought her to a halt beside the counter. She could not deny it; she was curious. Elizabeth turned around. An act she would regret for the rest of her life.

The Frenchman held in his hands a neatly folded pile of buttercup yellow brocade. Its raised pattern, an intriguing tangle of vines with thorns and blackberries, was woven of a soft buttery yellow. Elizabeth caught her breath and could not look away.

"Yes. I thought as much." He spoke softly, as if he were seducing her, unfurling the cloth onto the counter. "It is perfectly suited to your dark hair and the snowy cast of your skin. You and this silk were made for one another. Allow me to show you."

He turned her toward an oval mirror on the wall, and draped the cloth over her shoulder and under her chin. He was absolutely right. *Fascinating*. She ought to have been born wearing that color.

The Frenchman stood over her shoulder looking into the glass with her. "You see what I mean. It is—" He froze, frowning at something in the glass.

Elizabeth noticed it then, the reflection of a man outside the window peering in at them, Lord St. Cleve.

The merchant spun around. The silk, forgotten, sailed to the floor, brilliant warm yellow sliding across the dirty brown boards. Elizabeth clung to the length still draped over her shoulder.

The Frenchman, no longer charming and seductive, turned on Smythe full of anger. "You bastard! You betrayed me."

Elizabeth gasped at his sudden fury.

Smythe backed up, nearly crashing into the bins behind the counter. "What are you on about? I ain't betrayed no one."

"Then what is he doing here?" He gestured toward the window. Lord St. Cleve had turned away, but still stood out on the street. "I know this man." He spit on the floor, nearly striking the yellow silk. "Did you think his feeble disguise would fool me? I do not easily forget a man who chases me halfway across the continent."

Smythe's voice squeaked with fear. "I know nothing of disguises. Don't know who he is, I tell you."

Elizabeth shook her head, trying to comprehend the man's anger. She was certain it was Lord St. Cleve standing outside the shop. "Mr. Smythe is right. You've mistaken the man's identity."

"No mistake. One does not forget the Red Hawk." The silk merchant, who now appeared to be anything but simple, pulled a pistol from the inside of his coat and leveled it at Smythe. "Sniveling traitor. How much did the king's henchmen pay you, eh? Thirty pieces of silver? I hope you will enjoy it in hell."

Smythe shook his head, continuing to back up. "No! Merót, for pity's sake. Why would I peach on you? I'm perfectly satisfied with the blunt you—"

Merót fired. Elizabeth jumped. The blast reverberated through the room, ringing in her ears. Smythe slammed sideways, sliding to the floor. Eyes

wide, surprised. Red, the color of smashed strawberries, trickled out of his chest, faster, faster. Deaf.
Dumb. She stood paralyzed. Acrid smoke stung her
lungs. A sound came from her mouth. *Ladies do not
bellow.* Yet . . . Elizabeth screamed. And screamed.
Until yellow fabric twisted around her neck, shutting off the sound.

Silk, made especially for her, crushed her throat,
choking her to silence. The silk merchant's voice
mixed with the ringing in her ear. "You led him
here, didn't you? Spying for the Hawk. Didn't he
warn you? I do not tolerate deceit. Ever. If I had
time to reload, you would already be dead."

He twisted the fabric tighter, arching her backward. Elizabeth's head throbbed. The ceiling turned
gray and a million tiny dots of light fluttered around
the edges. Blood pounded at her temples. Banging.
Banging. Thumping. Struggling to keep from drowning in the watery gray realm of unconsciousness,
she heard wood splinter. The silk merchant swore
and shoved her to the floor.

Elizabeth gasped, tearing at the coiled cloth
around her neck, and coughed as air rushed back
into her lungs.

"Izzie!"

"Valen," she gasped. "Thank God."

St. Cleve lifted her to her knees and yanked away
the rest of the yellow silk. "Izzie? Can you breathe?"

She nodded.

"You're certain?"

As reason returned, she knew what must be done.
She fell forward, clutching his shoulders, wheezing
her desperate plea beside his cheek. "You must
catch him." She pointed at the curtain.

He held her in one arm and pushed a lock of

hair out of her eyes. "I can't leave you. You've been hurt."

She shook her head. "No. You must. I beg you." She struggled to breathe evenly enough to convince him. "Please."

"Right." He wasted no time dashing through the curtained doorway.

Elizabeth sank back on her haunches, still fighting to regulate her breathing and slow down her mad heartbeat.

She glanced up when someone whistled softly. "Cor' bless me. If this isn't a fine pickle." The stranger roamed in through the fractured door.

"Summon the ward, or a constable," she ordered.

"Bit late for that I'd say. I am the constable, miss." He warily approached Mr. Smythe and stooped to check for a pulse. "He's dead, he is." He frowned at her. "A bit of a tangle, this." He rubbed at his chin, clearly uncertain as to how to proceed. "Not a simple thing. Not as if your purse has been nabbed, now is it? No. Bit more complicated. I expect the magistrate will want Bow Street for a job like this."

"Well, don't stand there jabbering about it. Summon Bow Street. And hurry! Lord St. Cleve is chasing the madman by himself. If you delay too long, there may very well be two murders rather than one."

Elizabeth winced. It was the truth. What had possessed her to beg St. Cleve to chase after the murderer? He might very well end up in the same condition as Mr. Smythe. She grabbed her reeling head, fighting an urge to be sick.

How had she expected Valen to apprehend a lunatic? A lunatic with a pistol? She gingerly touched her bruised throat. Her heart began thumping un-evenly again. Why had she sent him into certain danger? Because, God forgive her, she was afraid. Every instinct she possessed screamed out in fear that Merót would return and finish what he started.

Those wretched tiny sparks at the edges of her vision returned, flickering in a whirling cloud. She vaguely heard the constable order one of the young lads peeping in the doorway to hurry off to Bow Street and call for a Runner. It seemed like a perfectly good time to swoon.

Chapter 12

Looming Considerations

When Elizabeth awakened, St. Cleve was carrying her into a soothing white room. "Are we dead?"

"Not I," he answered cryptically. "And you?"

His sarcasm was oddly reassuring. Elizabeth began to recognize her surroundings. They were entering Alison Hall. "I fainted?"

"So it would seem." He carried her up the stairs.

"But . . . I'm not the swooning type."

"I hadn't thought so."

Yet, she had fainted, and instantly recalled the reason why. Panic reared up in her throat, gagging her. "Did you catch him?"

There were no dimples to relieve the hard lines of his face. "No. But you must not think about that for the moment. Try to breathe evenly."

Don't think about it, she ordered herself. Never think about it. And yet, she could not escape. The images of it repeated themselves over and over in her mind. They finally reached the top of the stairs and the familiar hallway leading to her room. Leaning against his chest, she forced herself to take regular breaths instead of the great gulps she was wont to do.

St. Cleve laid her on her bed, and it seemed as if the entire household had followed them. A handful of servants buzzed around them and Lady Alameda stood in the doorway.

"What in heaven's name happened to her?" She had her hands on her hips and looked quite vexed. "She's as white as my boiled egg, which is, at this very moment, downstairs getting cold." She pointed at the doorway and then used the same finger to shake at them. "Why ever do you two engage in these early morning exercises? I cannot recommend vigorous activity before breakfast. And here's my proof, I daresay, the poor child fainted for want of sustenance."

St. Cleve dropped into the chair across from the bed. "No. It took a good deal more than missing her breakfast to do the job. But, what say you, Lady Elizabeth? Would you care to have a plate of eggs and fish brought to your room?"

The very thought made Elizabeth's stomach lurch. She scrunched up her nose and turned her head, pressing a hand against her lips.

Valen addressed his aunt. "I believe that will have to suffice for, 'Thank you very much, but no, I would prefer weak tea and toast.' "

Lady Alameda ignored him and demanded, "What happened? Where have you been?"

"Shopping," Valen answered enigmatically.

Elizabeth rubbed at her forehead, trying to make sense of it all. "How did we get back here?"

"I didn't carry you the whole way if that's what you're worried about. I hired a hack."

She turned up her nose again. "No wonder I smell so dreadful."

He snorted as if she were a silly child. "No, my dear. It would seem you and your brother have equally fragile stomachs. During the ride home, you would awaken screaming and, well . . . let us say, you ought to be deuced hungry. What little there was, is no longer with you."

Egad! She closed her eyes, horridly embarrassed. "Oh dear. I am not the sort who . . ."

"So you say." He shrugged. "It is to be expected under the circumstances."

"What circumstances?" Lady Alameda stamped her foot. "I expect a full report, Valen. I am not accustomed to being left in the dark in matters pertaining to members of my own household."

"Your household, alone?" He quizzed her. "My dear aunt, you do not like to be in the dark concerning matters pertaining to anyone in England, I should think. Indeed, I was surprised you did not have one of your informers standing outside Smythe and Sons."

Lady Alameda frowned at him. "Hmph. How very amusing you are. I'll see to arranging for Lady Elizabeth's weak broth and toast, shall I?"

Elizabeth felt a gnawing in her stomach. "And jam? If you please?"

"How delightful. Her appetite appears to be returning." Lady Alameda waved her fingers as she left the room.

Robert dashed into Elizabeth's room as soon as Lady Alameda left. His hair was tousled and his cuffs untied. "What's all the racket about? Servants said there'd been an accident. Are you hurt?"

"No."

"Then what are you doing in bed at this hour? And in your street clothes?"

"A scold? From my slug-a-bed brother who prefers to sleep until noon?"

He ran his fingers through his unruly hair. "Well, something's amiss, I know it. Had a dreadful night. Kept hearing screaming in my head."

Valen stretched out his long legs and rested one hand behind his neck, massaging the base as though Robert's mention of screams brought the chaotic events of the morning back down upon him. "Your sister witnessed a murder this morning."

"A murder? Gad! Izzie what happened?" Robert glanced from her to the surrounds of the room as though he expected to find evidence of the crime in her bedroom.

"Don't be daft. Not here." She turned away from him to stare out the window.

"Well, for pity's sake, tell me what happened."

"I don't want to talk about it."

Valen cleared his throat. "Unfortunately, my lady, there are a host of interested parties. A constable. Bow Street. The magistrate. All are quite eager to have your version of the events. They only allowed me to extract you from the scene on the promise that I would report, in minute detail, any information you might be able to give. Were it not for your inclination to swoon and to—"

"Yes. You mentioned that already." Elizabeth didn't want to hear it again.

"What?" Robert demanded.

"Cascaded." Valen answered evenly.

She groaned.

"Oh, I see, fainted *and* retched. Didn't know Izzie was the sort."

"No. I wouldn't have thought it either."

She punched her pillow and tried to get comfortable. "May we please change the subject?"

"Yes. You can jolly well tell me what happened. Let us begin with where you were?" Her brother's commanding tone surprised Elizabeth.

Still, he had no right to order her about, not after the morning she'd had. "I'm not ready to speak of it."

Robert swelled up and she recognized the imperious tone that her father used to take. "Izzie—" he warned.

"Your brother is right," Valen cut in. "Regrettably, there is urgency, my dear. The blighter who shot Smythe is still running loose in the city." He tapped his finger against the arm of the chair. "And there appears to be several circumstances surrounding the crime that are of particular interest to the officials."

She groaned, guessing exactly which circumstances those might be. What would happen when the magistrate discovered she'd been consorting with a smuggler, or worse, a thief? "I can't. I really can't"

"Unfortunately, if I do not carry your story to them with some haste, I have no doubt the authorities will arrive here shortly to interview you themselves."

"I need some laudanum."

"No," Robert ordered. "Won't have it. Not you, Izzie. You detest it when mother hides behind the stuff. Tell us what happened and have done with it."

She turned her face toward the pillow, afraid to look at either of them. "First, you must tell me what the penalty is for consorting with a smuggler."

The bed bounced as Robert sat down ungracefully on the edge. "I've no idea. Valen?"

"An innocent young lady, unaware of who she was dealing with—I doubt it will attract anyone's notice. The important thing is to get to the facts of the murder."

She sat up. "That's just it. I wasn't innocent. Mr. Smythe told me he had connections to a very exclusive source of French silks. I knew, full well, he meant a smuggler."

"Bah." Robert waved his hand at her. "You are astonishingly green at times. Duffers say that sort of thing in that district all the time, Izzie. Cheats who sell spitalfield goods at double their worth, pretending the wares are smuggled. Never say you fell for it?"

She glared at her arrogant brother. "I am not an idiot, Robert! This wasn't some toothless vendor standing on a corner. And these were, most assuredly, *not* common silks. Quite the contrary—I have rarely seen goods of such superb quality."

She motioned to Lord St. Cleve for confirmation. "You saw the fabric. Tell him."

"I didn't have time to examine them." He seemed a million miles away, absently rubbing the stubble on his cheek.

"Then you will both have to take my word on the matter."

St. Cleve dropped the point entirely. "The murderer, Lady Elizabeth, what do you remember about him? I only saw the back of his head. He turned toward the window, so I was forced to step away."

"Aha! So you were spying on me."

St. Cleve waved away her accusation. "I followed you. Merely a matter of concern for your safety. A young woman, unaccompanied, leaving the house so early in the morning—"

"You followed me."

He frowned at her diversion. "The murderer, Lady Elizabeth. What do you remember?"

Too much. Far too much. The elegant taper of his fingers as he held the cloth to her throat. Every nuance of his voice, each minute inflection of his accent as he told her she would die. The hateful glimmer in his brown eyes as he choked her. She gently touched the tender bruise at her neck. *How will I ever forget?* "He was French," she mumbled.

Robert smacked the bedcovers and snorted at her impatiently. "Well, naturally, he would be, wouldn't he?"

She turned to Lord St. Cleve. "He thought he knew you. Which was rubbish, of course. I tried to tell him. When he saw your reflection in the mirror, it completely unhinged him." Elizabeth hesitated. "He was a madman, I suppose. He called you by an odd name." She tilted her head, noticing how very alert St. Cleve's eyes were, and the sharp line of his nose. "He called you the Red Hawk."

Valen and Robert turned to one another, their expressions laden with alarm.

"What?" she demanded. *They will not keep secrets from me.* "What is it?"

Valen said nothing, but glanced away, pretending to study the gray clouds outside the window.

Robert traced a design on the bedcovers with his finger.

"Did this man give you his name?" Valen's tone was stern, commanding.

"I asked it. He avoided telling me, saying he was merely a *simple merchant.* I didn't believe him—his manners were too refined, his speech too elegant. Later, when Mr. Smythe begged him for his life, Mr. Smythe called the man Merót."

Robert clutched the bedcovers in his fist. Valen turned and stared at her, his jaw flexing so hard she could see the muscles tighten from where she lay.

"What is it? Tell me. You must!" She sat up. "When he was choking me, he called me a spy. Absurd, isn't it? Me?" She laughed, nervous, wishing they would laugh, too, and tell her it was all a mad joke. "He said you should have warned me about what he does to spies. For pity's sake . . ."

Valen stood up, towering over her, his face hard, unyielding. *How in heaven's name did I ever mistake him for a fop?*

"There is no time. I must deliver your report to Whitehall."

"Whitehall? But . . . I thought the magistrate—"

"Robert, stay with your sister."

Her brother nodded gravely as Valen strode toward the door.

Elizabeth leaned over and tugged on her brother's arm. "You must explain. You must. My whole world is turning topsy-turvy."

St. Cleve paused at the door, his back to them. "Robert, I trust you will remember your oath. For her sake as well as for others."

Robert sighed heavily. "It pains me that you should doubt it."

St. Cleve left without another word, and Elizabeth knew her brother would remain mum no matter how much she cajoled him. "Since you're not going to explain to me why I nearly had the life squeezed out of me today. I believe I will have some of that laudanum, thank you."

He chucked her chin and got up from the bed. "None was offered."

"Hmph." She threw the pillow at him.

Chapter 13

Making A Silk Officer Out of a Fop's Purse

Valen strode hurriedly to his rooms, rang for Biggs, and sat down in a chair in front of the mirror. Biggs ran up the stairs, bounding through the door, huffing and puffing. "The servants are humming like bees. What happened? I knew I should've come w' you."

Valen handed his sergeant a pair of scissors. "Cut off my hair."

Biggs took the shears and stared at Valen as if he couldn't entirely comprehend the order.

Valen reached back and pulled loose the leather thong tying back his unruly mop. "Cut my hair."

"Aye, I heard you. But Captain, folding clothes and laundering is one thing. Cutting hair, that's something else altogether."

"Good grief, man. It isn't as if I'm asking you to carve a statue of Nelson for Trafalgar Square; just cut it short and trim. And after you do, pull out

the good clothes. No more of this fribble business."

"It's that glad I am to hear it, my lord. High time
you showed these folks what's what. But I expect
you'll be wanting someone else to chop that hair
down for you. Unless, of course, you don't mind it
looking somewhat like this." He yanked off his wig.

Valen frowned at the scraggily clumps of hair
hanging around the edges of Biggs balding pate.
He stood up and retied his long hair into the
leather thong. "Yes, well, I believe we will forego
the haircut for the nonce. However, as soon as possible, both of us will make a trip to the barber. For
now, do you think you might manage to find me
something civilized to wear to Whitehall?"

"Whitehall?" Biggs cocked his head.

"Yes. You know, cravat, black coat, that sort of
thing."

"I know that, sir. But what's to do at the govern-
ment offices?"

"It would seem our old friend, Merót, is in
London."

Biggs stared openmouthed before cursing
roundly. "The devil, you say."

"Precisely."

Late that night, or rather, very early in the
morning, Valen slipped quietly through the front
door at Alison Hall, exhausted, but not wishing to
disturb the servants. It had been a hellish sort of
night. The war office had issued him fifty men to
do a job that easily might have utilized three hundred. He'd set them to scouring the docks and
wharfs, searching every outgoing ship in port, and
questioning landlords and innkeepers. Around

midnight, they thought they had located Merót's lodgings.

With a dozen men, Valen had rushed into a tenement in Blackfriars. They had burst through the door and found the small room vacated. He could almost smell the bloody Frenchman. Merót's cologne was not musk or sandalwood, like most gentlemen wore, but a spicy floral scent, almost feminine; it clawed at Valen's nostrils, sickening him. The bed had been fastidiously made up, and in the corner lay a stack of neatly folded silks. Valen had angrily shoved the chair posed at a perfect right angle to Merót's desk.

He had organized a net of men encircling Blackfriars and the surrounding streets. No one could come in or go out without his men searching them. He had also positioned men at the docks. They had waited in vain. Merót was probably tucked up in bed somewhere snickering at their ineffectual attempts to catch him. Valen had changed out his sentries at three o'clock and had decided he might as well drag home and get some rest.

Locking the door, he strode quietly up the marble stairs. Moonlight slid through the glass dome illuminating the rotunda with soothing silver light. Valen needed a few hours of solid rest before renewing his search in the morning. He felt certain the Frenchman must have slipped through his grasp, the net was simply a precaution, but with the ports sealed off, where would he go? Would he try to flee England? Or would he . . .

Merót's history of vengeance gnawed at Valen. He remembered all too well the tortured bodies of many of their paid informers. Some of Valen's men ordered to follow Merót and track movements from a distance had fallen prey to his knife or pistol. The bastard always left their bodies with a mocking message for the Red Hawk. Valen should have disregarded orders and killed the madman long ago.

Valen stepped onto the second floor landing when he heard her scream. A soft cry, muffled. Then louder. He raced up the next set of stairs to Elizabeth's room and threw open the door. She screamed again, a breathy helpless noise, as if the throat would not allow the sound to take full force. Pure panic.

He scoured the shadows as he rushed to her side, and saw nothing out of place. "What is it?" he demanded, taking hold of her shoulders. He saw none of the familiar arrogance in her face, no pride, just ravaging fear.

She gulped for air, gasping, and pointed toward the window. He saw nothing there. In his most soothing voice he asked, "What was it? Tell me. What did you see?"

Her shoulders quaked in his hands. "Him. In the window."

A nightmare. He understood then, and hugged her against his chest, petting her hair. "Shhh. It's gone. You're safe now." He would make certain she was safe. Her quivering subsided as he held her and stroked her hair and back. He listened, waiting for her breathing to calm down.

She clung to Valen as if her life depended on it. "I saw him. At my window. Come to finish killing me. I know it."

"Shhh. Breathe, Izzie. I'm not in a mood to have you cascade down the front of my shirt just now."

That did it. She let go of him and leaned away, leaving his arms feeling regrettably empty. "You don't believe me?"

It nearly broke his heart, the expression on her face. He'd wounded her. "I believe you thought you saw something."

Her brow pinched together. "I did see him."

He nodded, unwilling to upset her any further. As she labored under the weight of so many emotions, her breasts rose and fell, innocent of the enticing effect it had on him. Gad, she was bewitching. Silver light floated over her, touching her hair and skin as he only dreamed of doing. He brushed back a tendril of black hair from her cheek. "You've been through far too much today. You must rest."

"He's going to kill me." She lowered her eyes.

He lifted her chin in his hand. "I won't let that happen."

She met his gaze. "I would think you'd only be too . . ."

He appreciated that she had the good sense not to finish the ridiculous statement, but he did it for her. ". . . glad to be rid of you." He trailed his fingers over her cheek. "You cannot really think so?"

He left the question hanging and leaned toward her lips, capturing them in his. He did not plunder her mouth as he had last time. Although, he knew instinctively she would let him, even welcome it. Knowing made him ache all the more to do it, but he held back. He kissed her as softly as the moonlight he was so jealous of, gently touching her full lips with his, scarcely holding her in his hands, leaving her the freedom to escape his grasp, or his kiss, at any time if she willed it.

She did neither.

When he reluctantly pulled away from her mouth, he realized he had completely forgotten to breathe. Now he was the one gasping, desperate. *Reckless behavior. Foolish.* Unfortunately, his treacherous body was ordering him to do it again, and unless he beat a hasty retreat, he would not be able to resist.

"Come." He stood up and pulled her to her feet. "I want to show you something." Valen led her to the window and unlocked the sash, swinging it open, and then he leaned out. The cool night air blew some sense into his wobbling brain. "Take a look down here."

She peeked nervously over the edge.

"Do you see? It's three stories down."

"I know that. But I've heard stories of thieves and brigands who can climb—"

He nodded. "Up drain pipes and trellises. There is neither a drain, nor a trellis outside your window."

"But, his face, I saw it so clearly. Right here. I woke up. It sounded as if someone were fiddling with the latch. And there he was, outside the glass. Here."

Valen stared out of the window, squinting into the darkness, wondering if the ledge under her casement was wide enough to hold a deranged French spy.

Robert straggled into the room in his night-dress, carrying a candle. "What's all the to do? Kept hearing screams in my sleep again. I swear, Izzie, I should have left you home with mama. Never should have tried to bring you to town. Too much bother."

She sniffed, and the tip of her nose made its familiar journey toward the ceiling. "Very nice. Considering I am the one with the plan to keep us out of the river tick."

"You and your plans. This is another superb example of what happens when I listen to your schemes." Robert set the candle down and dropped unceremoniously into the chair at her bedside. "And what are you doing here, Valen? Devil take it. Do I need to call you out for being in my sister's room in the middle of the night?"

Valen and Izzie exchanged guilty glances.

The truth always being the best option, Valen launched into a full frontal attack of honesty. "Yes. Go ahead then, call me out. Undoubtedly, I deserve it. You know all too well that I'm not much of a stickler on the proprieties. Alluring chit, your sister. Thought I'd just dash into her room and have my way with her after a busy night of chasing Merót around London. A pity she had a nightmare and ruined the mood."

Izzie looked up at him in alarm.

Valen winked at her. "What say you, Robert, pistols at dawn? Perhaps I might persuade you to postpone until dawn two days from now? I'm devilish tired."

Robert appeared to be half dozing in the chair. "Right. I take it Merót got away then, the slippery bugger. Sorry, Izzie. Pardon my language."

"He did." Valen tugged Elizabeth back toward the bed. "I was just showing your sister that he could not possibly have been the apparition she saw outside her window. Three stories up. No drain pipe or trellis."

Robert propped his head in his hand. "I dunno. Wouldn't put it past him. Clever devil, our Merót."

Valen wanted to smack his friend in the head. "In that case, I hope you find that chair comfortable. You will stay here in her room with her, to make certain there are no more apparitions at her window."

Robert groaned.

Izzie climbed under the bedsheets and Valen reached up to tuck them down. His hand grazed against a foreign fabric under her pillow. He tugged at it, and leaned over her to get a glimpse of it. In the flickering light of Robert's candle he recognized the edge of a sleeve sewn of green brocade, a green brocade decorated with peacocks and trimmed in hideous orange satin.

My coat. He would have laid odds she had burned the thing. Valen stared at Izzie, trying to sort it out. She smiled up at him. Then, as it dawned on her what he'd discovered, her expression turned to dread. She turned to see his hand beside her pillow and groaned. Rolling quickly onto her side, she jerked the fabric away from him and stuffed it back under her pillow.

Robert thumped his hand angrily against the arm of the chair. "I should have known!"

They looked at him. Valen feared his confounded desire for Izzie must be a palpable thing. Robert really would have to call him out if he could read his thoughts at this moment.

Izzie's voice arced up a trifle too high. "Should have known what?"

"Merót! When he disappeared on the continent—I should have guessed he'd come here. But no, I assumed he'd hared off to Russia."

Izzie and Valen both relaxed.

"Might have puzzled it out, too, if I hadn't gotten called home. What the devil has he been up to?"

Valen stood up and paced to the window. "His old game, I expect, advising Napoleon's generals on the movements of our troops."

"But how?"

"We discussed it at length in the war office today.

If we have guessed correctly, Merót's scheme was relatively simple. Officers have sisters, sweethearts, mothers. These women buy silk. You know how charming he can be." Valen glanced furtively at Elizabeth, who refused to look in his direction.

He continued, "Suppose he ingratiates himself to a lady who wishes to purchase his silk. In the course of conversation, this lady mentions she has received a letter from her sweetheart, or son, who is marching, let us say, toward Madrid. Merót, merely by expressing a casual interest, might easily extract more information regarding troop movement without her becoming the least suspicious."

Izzie sat up, startled. "You may be right!" She glanced from Valen to her brother. "Not three weeks ago, just as I entered the shop, Mr. Smythe escorted Lady Cauvil out from behind his curtain. At the time, I thought it odd that she should be in a back room, alone with a shopkeeper. But she probably wasn't, was she? Merót must have been there. Smythe handed her a package, and she nodded amiably to me as if nothing were amiss. I forgot all about it until now." Izzie looked expectantly at her brother. "You realize, don't you, Lady Cauvil has a younger son who is with Wellington in Spain."

Robert nodded. "That's it then. That must be his game. We'll want a chat with Lady Cauvil."

"Yes." Valen pulled the window shut and latched it. "However, on the morrow, I think it would be prudent to move your sister to more distant territory, for both her peace of mind and her safety."

Izzie met his gaze. "So you do think he'll find me and finish what he started."

"No. It's merely a precaution until we capture him." Valen hated to lie to her. Maybe it wasn't a lie. Maybe Merót wouldn't bother to slake his revenge with so much at risk.

"Could take her home, I suppose." Robert rubbed his chin thoughtfully.

"He knew my name." She laid her head down, eyes drooping, her voice growing airy and soft with fatigue. "If he finds I'm not in London, I should think our estate would be the first place he'd look."

"Gad. She's right. And there's no one there but our mum and a few old servants, too faithful to abandon us, but hardly useful in a skirmish."

Valen turned to Robert. "We'll take her to Ransley Keep. He'd never think of looking there, and my father will be glad of the company. Pack and be ready to leave at daybreak. And now, I must excuse myself for a few hours of much needed rest."

"See here, Valen. I'm terribly grateful and all." Robert stood up blocking Valen's escape. "But you don't really need me to travel with you, do you? What's the point of two escorts? Much better if I stay here. Help the lads hunt him down. After all, I studied Merót for two years. Would still have had him in my sights if I hadn't been summoned home on account of my blasted fa—" He cast an uneasy look in his sister's direction.

Father. The same reason Valen had been required to return to England—to take his place as head of the family. One father missing. One dying. Their families left in tatters. Both men studied Elizabeth. This is who they came home for, the innocent who needed their protection. She lay drifting to sleep.

"Very well," he said softly. "I'll leave Biggs to assist you. Without a doubt, Whitehall will be pleased to have your assistance. I advised them you were in town. And I'll return as soon as Elizabeth is situated." Valen clapped a hand on Robert's shoulder. "But are you certain you aren't choosing to stay here because of a certain Miss Dunworthy?"

Robert chuckled. "Not a bit of it."

"Hmm. Try to remember this is serious business we're engaged in."

"Don't know what you mean, Captain. What business are you referring to, Miss Dunworthy or Merót?"

He smirked at his friend's wry wit. "Both."

"Too true."

Valen turned to go, but at the door, he paused for one last look at Izzie sleeping with her arms wrapped tightly around her pillow, his hideous peacock coat tucked underneath. Something in his chest constricted. He found it hard to swallow. "I meant it, Robert. Stay here with her until I can get her safely away."

Robert inhaled deeply, almost as if it vexed him that he must play sentinel, but he dropped willingly into the chair beside his sister. His face, a mirror image of the concern besieging Valen.

Chapter 14

A Kitten Tangled in the Yarn

It was not daybreak when they departed. Owing largely to the fact that Aunt Honore insisted on coming along, hours of preparation consumed the entire morning. Valen paced angrily in the rotunda, checking his pocket watch every ten minutes. It was well into the afternoon when they climbed into the coach, which meant the journey would cost Valen an extra day.

Aunt Honore sat opposite him, beside Elizabeth, and had the decency to wait until they were well underway before making demands. "Change places with me, Valen."

He glanced caustically in her direction, purposely elevating one eyebrow. "I'm quite comfortable where I am, thank you."

"Well, I am not. I prefer a seat to myself."

"No one forced you to come along."

She shrugged. "Couldn't very well have left Lady Elizabeth to ride alone in a closed carriage with you, could I?"

"I would have ridden outside," he drawled as if she were a slow-witted child.

Honore smacked her white-gloved hand against the black leather seat. "Humbug. It's a five-hour journey. You would have been exceedingly uncomfortable up on the roof."

"I've weathered considerably longer treks, and under worse conditions," he muttered to no one in particular, knowing he may as well talk to the ceiling for all the heed she would give him.

"Oh, do stop grumbling and change places. I don't want Lady Elizabeth drooling on me."

That remark claimed Lady Elizabeth's attention. She turned from the window. "I assure you, my lady, I do not drool. I would not dream of—"

Honore waved her hand through the air as if she were shooing away fireflies. "Bound to fall asleep, aren't you? I slipped some laudanum into your tea this morning."

Valen frowned at his aunt.

"You didn't!" Izzie's mouth did that opening and shutting thing she was wont to do from time to time.

"Of course, I did."

"But surely, you should have asked me first. My brother will have apoplexy. He hates the stuff. Thinks I will become addicted like my—"

"Oh, don't fret, my dear." She patted Elizabeth's leg. "Your brother is much too young for apoplexy. The most he will do is climb up in the boughs about it."

Valen crossed his arms and snorted derisively.

"You will have to pardon my aunt. Her behavior is guided solely by calculating what she might get away with. She's entirely without scruples."

"I have scruples."

"Not many."

"Just enough."

"Well, you ought not to have dosed Lady Elizabeth without asking."

"Piffle. It was a very light dose. See here." She cupped her hand under Elizabeth's chin and inspected her closely. "She isn't even drooping yet. Her eyes are only a little glazed. After hearing an account of her histrionics yesterday, I certainly didn't intend to spend the journey watching her get sick and mopping up—"

Elizabeth groaned and pulled out of her grasp. "I assure you, I do not normally suffer in that regard. There were . . . extraordinary circumstances."

Aunt Honore smoothed out her purple traveling dress. "I preferred not to take the chance."

Valen regarded his aunt's haughty demeanor, knowing full well she was maneuvering him. "All the more reason why you ought to have remained at Alison Hall."

"Nonsense. High time I saw my brother again. He will want a report on how you are coming along. Let me see . . ." She tapped her lips and glanced pointedly at Elizabeth and then back to him. "Whatever shall I tell him? How are you coming along with your promise, Valen dear?"

Cunning ploy. He had no wish to apprise Elizabeth of the matter. His aunt was, indeed, unscrupulous. "Very well, I will change places with you. Here. Take my seat. But, for pity's sake, spare me any more of your jabber."

Honore switched places with him and plopped

down triumphantly, looking from Valen to Izzie. "Do try not to drool on my nephew, Lady Elizabeth. It is the first time he has worn something presentable in recent memory."

"I shall endeavor to do my best." Izzie inclined her head graciously, but he caught the hint of mirth in the set of her lips. She stoically sat upright as if her back were still tied to a board from her youth.

By the time they reached the outskirts of London, Elizabeth had, indeed, succumbed to the laudanum. She tipped sideways and flopped against the squibs.

Honore sighed lamentably and pointed at Izzie. "Only look at the poor gel, Valen, bumping her head against the side of the coach. It gives me the megrims just to watch. Can you not arrange for her to lean against something more comfortable? Your shoulder, perhaps?"

He fixed her with a level stare. "Usually your conspiracies are not so thinly disguised."

"Whatever can you mean?"

He didn't bother to answer, merely removed his coat and folded it into a bundle to use as a cushion for Elizabeth's head.

"Oh, for pity's sake, don't crumple up your coat." Honore groaned. "I liked that one."

But, when Valen leaned over to prop it under Izzie's head she moved into his embrace, draping herself against his chest, nestling up to him like a kitten to a mother cat.

Honore grinned triumphantly. "Well done, Valen."

"You are completely incorrigible."

"So I've been told."

Valen surrendered to his predicament, dropped his coat on the seat and rested his arm around Izzie. She fit neatly against his side as if she was designed for the purpose. The gentle rhythm of her breathing tickled his chest, promising that he would not easily ignore her presence. To the contrary, he could not think of anything but her body pressed up against his.

Peculiar, how tucking a woman up against a man makes him feel things he might otherwise avoid. Judging by his aunt's smug expression, she had known precisely what effect it would have on him.

"Would it be so very terrible, Valen?" Honore asked, as if reading his mind.

Devious woman. He refused to answer. Instead, Valen studied the landscape as it drifted past the window in peaceful predictable formations, fields of sheep and grain, familiar hills, the same ancient villages that had stood there since the days of King Henry. He was going home to Ransley Keep. His heart softened with a vague eagerness. *Home.* And somehow, it seemed far more inviting because Izzie lay next to him, snuggled up against his chest.

Toward the end of the journey, Elizabeth roused, groping to find her way out of a cloying deep dark cavern. Slowly, the air around her became more real. Awareness seeped in gradually. With a grimace, she realized her face was pressed up, rather indecorously, against Lord St. Cleve's broad chest. Elizabeth sat up abruptly, checking the condition of her hair, straightening her traveling dress, blinking at the dimming light. Evening approached. "I must have dozed off."

"To be sure." Lady Alameda nodded.

Valen pinched the fabric of his shirt, pulling it away from his skin and arched his brow at her. "It would seem, my lady, that you do indeed drool."

She stared at the embarrassingly large moisture stain trailing down from where her mouth had been pressed against him. What could she say? Nothing for it. "You must send me the laundering bill." She smiled.

A short time later, their coach turned down a bumpy country lane, and at long last, rolled to a stop. St. Cleve held Elizabeth's hand as she stepped down from the carriage and stared up at Ransley Keep.

A mammoth old manor sat on a hill. It looked more like a fortress than a house. Dark stone walls lent it an impenetrable appearance. Flags waved from a small parapet. One could easily envision medieval archers lined up across the battlements at the top. In the waning light, Elizabeth felt transported back to a time when swords clanked together and arrows whistled through the air as lords fought to protect their families and lands.

She shook her head. Perhaps, she was still experiencing the effects of the laudanum.

"Magical, isn't it?" Lady Alameda stood beside her. "The original castle is a crumbling ruin on another hill. One of my ancestors built this, trying to be faithful in spirit to the old keep. Come. You must meet my brother."

Valen put a restraining hand on his aunt's shoulder. "Lord Ransley will be resting. We should not intrude upon him until tomorrow morning."

"Nonsense! He'll be eager to see you *and* to meet Lady Elizabeth. If he's sleeping, we'll wake him."

"I insist you do not excite him in regard to Lady Elizabeth. We must not alarm him concerning . . . recent events."

"Don't be silly." Lady Alameda tossed her head

imperiously. "I have no intention of alarming him on that account."

"On *any* account," Valen ordered.

Honore rolled her eyes and trudged through the heavy doors that a servant had creaked open.

Chapter 15

The Flimsy Fabric of Prevarication

Elizabeth oversaw the unpacking of her luggage and took time to wash away the travel dust before meeting Lord Ransley. She marveled at the castle-like quality of her bedroom. The architect had left the stone walls and heavy wooden beams exposed, just as he had throughout the rest of the manor. She removed her traveling dress and changed into a light green sprigged muslin. As she tiptoed down the broad open stairs into the great hall below, she felt like a fairy princess in an ancient stronghold.

She waited in the great room by the fireplace, studying a large old coat of arms hanging above it. The shield was partitioned into six sections. One, no doubt a grant from Queen Elizabeth, contained a white field with three red falcons, each holding a rose in his raised claw. *The Red Hawk. Arms for St. Cleve?*

Engrossed in her study, she didn't hear Valen approach. "A hodgepodge, is it not?"

She started and spun around; almost colliding with him, he stood so close. "The hawks . . . ?" His nearness flustered her so much she couldn't put her question together properly.

He shrugged.

Rather than dressing up for the occasion of seeing his father, St. Cleve had donned a pair of nankeen trousers, more suited for riding than the drawing room, and a plain cambric shirt with no neck cloth. Then she remembered. "I do apologize for ruining your only dress shirt, my lord."

"Small matter. My father would be alarmed if I were to put on my best bib and tucker for a mere visit. He might think he'd passed and was a ghost at his own funeral. Surely, nothing else could induce me to put on finery at home."

Before Elizabeth could sort out his entire meaning, he had her on his arm, leading her up the stairs again. "Hurry. With any luck we will arrive in his room before my aunt does."

Lord Ransley's bedroom was dark. It smelled of close fetid air and a heavy cologne that must have been sprinkled liberally to mask the odor. Servants were lighting more candles as they entered. Lord Ransley sat up in bed, an eager expression on his face. "Valen, my boy, delighted to see you. And you've brought your bride! How lovely she is."

Valen's feet suddenly stuck to the floor. He clamped Elizabeth's hand in place on his arm with the strength of an iron shackle. She nearly stumbled; they came to such an abrupt stop. Elizabeth glanced sideways at him and saw the sheer panic on his face.

Apparently, the very notion of an alliance between the two of them struck Lord St. Cleve dumb with terror. *How very amusing. Insulting, but amusing.* It would have only required a small explanation to set the matter right with his father. But she decided he might jolly well extricate himself from this little tangle without any help from her.

"I . . . No. She's not my . . . We haven't . . ." The fact that the high and mighty, overconfident Lord St. Cleve stammered nearly moved her to laughter. All too quickly, he recovered and stiffened to attention. "Has Aunt Honore been here already?"

His father shook his head. "Honore? No." He gestured weakly in Elizabeth's direction. "She's not—?"

"No."

His father's countenance wilted.

St. Cleve urged her toward Lord Ransley's bedside. "That is to say . . . She's an acquaintance. A friend."

At least it did not put him to the blush to call her his friend. He presented Elizabeth to his father, leaving off her title, which she thought curious, but did not correct. She was, after all, his guest, and so she ought to cooperate with whatever subterfuge he deemed necessary.

"You promised." Lord Ransley raked his pale fingers through the wispy brown hair above his brow.

Valen stiffened. "I assure you, my lord, I will keep my word. All in good time."

"Sometime before the next age, I hope." Lord Ransley coughed, his chest heaving as he struggled to suppress a spasm. "I'd like to be here to see it."

Valen brightened. "That is the very reason I brought Miss Hampton to you. She is skilled with herbs. It is my hope she might strengthen your lungs with one of her concoctions."

Elizabeth stared at St. Cleve, wondering how he had divined her fascination with the medicinal characteristics of plants. However, she was not skilled by any stretch of the imagination, a mere novice at best. She tugged on his sleeve trying to admonish him to stop inflating her abilities.

His father's interest rekindled slightly. "You brought me an herbalist? A healer?"

St. Cleve grimaced. "Not a healer, precisely. She's versed in some herbal remedies, and aside from that, I thought you might enjoy her company. She has offered to play chess with you, read books, that sort of thing."

"Read to me? You brought a young lady here to read to me?" Lord Ransley's brows furrowed skeptically, glancing from one to the other as if he hoped to decipher their true objective.

Lady Alameda swished into the bedroom, her silk skirts rustling. "Ah, William! So, you've met our Lady Elizabeth."

"*Lady* Elizabeth? But—" Lord Ransley fell into a short paroxysm. "Valen said—"

"Told you everything, did he?"

St. Cleve inhaled noisily, flexed his jaw muscles and glared at his aunt.

His aunt completely disregarded his warning. "And did he mention that he's been chasing after some demented French spy who is on the rampage in London? Fellow hangs close to the shadows, I can tell you that. I had a devil of a time finding out more about him."

"A spy? What nonsense is this, Valen?" Lord

Ransley started to cough, but reached for a glass of water on the bed stand and sipped before continuing. "Are you putting yourself in danger again? We discussed this—"

Valen stepped in front of his aunt and placed a hand on his father's shoulder. "It's nothing. Don't trouble yourself over it. Truly. It is a small administrative affair I must finish up—nothing more."

Lady Alameda muttered under her breath, "Administrative affair, indeed. Is that what they call mur—"

He cut her off. "I told Lord Ransley that Elizabeth is versed in herbs and will try to ease some of his discomfort with her tonics."

"Her?" Lady Alameda edged around Valen. "Fiddle-faddle! Doubtful the gel knows a bluebell from a nightshade. Lucky thing if she doesn't poison him."

Elizabeth murmured that she most certainly did know the difference, but no one attended.

Lord Ransley rested deep in his pillows, shading his eyes against the candlelight. "This is all very confusing. When the servants told me Valen had come with a young lady in tow, naturally, I thought he'd found . . ." He glanced wistfully at Elizabeth. ". . . a wife to bring a measure of joy into his life."

Another cough shook his body, and then another followed. He sat up to manage the explosive surges from his lungs. The lace, at his throat and on his wrists, fluttered with each shuddering effort. He yanked a handkerchief from his sleeve and mopped his mouth, a dribble of blood at the corner of his lips remained. "I had hoped . . ." Too tired to finish the thought, Lord Ransley closed his eyes and lay back.

As he rested, Elizabeth could not help but observe the weary lines in his face that had been carved by too much pain. Obviously, Lord Ransley did not hide from his affliction by overusing opiates. To avoid suffering, he might well have drifted into a murky drug-induced land of nightmares and dreams that would cloud his pain—just as Elizabeth's mother had done to escape her troubles. Lord Ransley had enough courage and concern for his son to stay in the land of the living despite his pain. She wondered if Valen realized his good fortune.

Lady Alameda flicked her nephew on the arm.

"I gave you my word. I will keep it," Lord St. Cleve reminded his father, bristling as he did. "I should think that would suffice."

Lady Alameda flicked him again.

Elizabeth stepped back. Valen appeared to be nearing the limit of what he would tolerate.

In carefully measured tones, he reiterated, "It is not something that can be achieved in a day. It may require some time."

His aunt surveyed her fingernails. When she found them unharmed after all the flicking, she glanced up at her nephew, wearing a vengeful expression. "Unfortunately, Valen is proving rather thickheaded on that score. Seems your son imagines he might find his happiness with a lisping dodo bird rather than preferring someone who can play a decent game of chess."

"What?" Lord Ransley lifted his hand halfheartedly. "Can't fathom that. Lad needs a challenge." He turned to Valen. The gray circles ringing his eyes inspired compassion. They all leaned closer to hear what he might say. "Didn't you tell me this young lady plays chess?"

Honore grinned wickedly. "How very astute, William. I believe you are right."

"You are tired, my lord." Valen pulled Elizabeth back from the bed. "We will leave you to rest."

"You two run along." The countess's voice had a cheerful singsong quality as she shooed them out. "My brother and I have a great deal to catch up on."

Valen hesitated. If he could bodily pick up his aunt and haul her from the room without it upsetting his father, Elizabeth was certain he would do exactly that.

"He is tired, Aunt Honore." He issued it as an order, one that any soldier would have readily obeyed. "You must leave him."

"Nonsense. I've only just arrived."

Chapter 16

Ribbons and Garlic Balls, Tied up with Lace

Elizabeth awoke early the next morning, as was her habit, and glanced around the room, unable to remember where she was. In the faint light, she failed to recognize the tapestries on the wall or the massive carved bedposts. Was she waking or still dreaming? She sat up, clutching the coverlet. Then, she remembered. This was his home, Valen's home.

Slipping out of bed, she went to the window and tugged back the velvet curtain. Morning. The sun had not yet risen above the crimson horizon. Misty pink light melted over the land as it curved and undulated in delightful grassy pastures dotted with sheep and patches of yellowing grain. Each patch bounded by meandering rock walls and winding brooks. Perhaps she had fallen asleep and awakened in a previous century, for surely the land had looked exactly thus a hundred years ago, a land completely unaffected by the rigors and expectations of society. Elizabeth took a deep breath and tried not to envy Valen for that.

On a nearby hill, she spied the ruins of the old keep and decided that a bracing morning walk might clear her head from the effects of the opiates. But before she left, she dug a small rosewood recorder out of her trunk, a treasure from her childhood she always kept with her.

Elizabeth slipped quietly out of the manor house and into the welcoming morning air. Along the way, she stopped to pick some red clover flowers in the pastures, dropping them into the pocket of her serviceable old muslin walking dress, wondering if a tea made from the blossoms might not be used to strengthen Lord Ransley's lungs. Wandering in the direction of the old keep, she hoped to climb the hill and have a look at the crumbling stone walls, but the ruins proved to be farther away than she'd anticipated.

A brook, the width of a country lane, obstructed her path. Standing at the edge, she watched the ribbon of clear water ripple over stones and wash over moss as it hurried on its way. Here and there, minnows swam against the current and then allowed themselves to be carried along only to playfully battle their way back up stream.

With not one soul in sight, what harm could there be if she waded across and, perhaps, scooped up a handful of water to quench her thirst? *Ladies must not be seen without stockings and shoes.*

Elizabeth ignored the admonition of her former governess and quickly removed the requisite gear for ladies from her feet. She tiptoed onto a stone, balancing as a thin stream of cold water ran around her bare feet. She held up her skirts and laughed softly. Her next step missed and carried her into the water almost up to her calf. By the time she forded the little stream, she was shivering. Her shoes and stockings lay forgotten on the bank behind her as she climbed up onto a large rock and sat down to dry in the sun before crossing back.

It was a perfect morning. She took out her recorder and began to play. With each tune she played, her heart seemed lighter. The round notes of the recorder echoed against the vastness of the countryside, floating up, carrying away her troubles and fears.

Valen heard Elizabeth before he saw her, knowing the flute song must belong to her, rather than a shepherd. There was a complexity to the melody that spoke of her, a frivolous string of notes followed by a melancholy turn that caused his own heart to ache in response. But, as soon as the music touched him with despair, she altered the chords, replaying an airy childlike cadence.

From the hilltop, he spotted her and nudged Hercules down the rise. "Come on, boy. Care to have a look at the most bothersome female in all of Christendom?"

The big chestnut snorted and picked up his gait.

Izzie didn't seem to notice their approach. The scattered trees and bushes lining the little stream must have obscured her view. Valen guided Hercules to an opening in the growth across the creek from her and sat listening as she played. Her toes dangled naked over the edge of a boulder, waggling in rhythm to her convoluted tune, a tune that ended abruptly when she finally spotted him.

* * *

Elizabeth glanced up from fingering her flute, and nearly fell off the rock, startled. Across the creek, astride a huge red horse, Valen looked like an ancient raiding warlord. She realized, in that moment, what she had secretly known in her heart all along. He was quite possibly the most magnificent man on earth.

Small wonder he hid himself behind such ridiculous clothing. With his title and prospects, if he'd come to town dressed properly every female in London would have lined up to . . . And it was only a matter of time before they all discovered what now seemed so abundantly evident to Elizabeth.

What a blind ninny she'd been. Lord St. Cleve could have his choice of females, while she would be left with either a very rich mincing poet, or a wealthy cherubic coxcomb. If only her situation were different.

She wondered if St. Cleve might have a large allowance granted from his father. Not large, she amended, an enormous allowance. Or perhaps, there was a chance the income from his inheritance might suffice? *A very small chance.* Even so, how would she convince him that she suited? *Little hope of either.* He thought of her as an annoying marmot. Elizabeth let the recorder drop into her pocket, the music in her soul evaporated.

Valen prodded his mount forward, splashed into the brook, and picked his way carefully across the water and up the bank to her rock. He dismounted and stood beside her. "A fine morning, my lady." He wore no hat and had on a rough cambric shirt with the sleeves rolled up over the muscles of his arms as if he were a tenant farmer just come in from the fields.

She nodded and tried to smile, but it wouldn't work. She fought back an overpowering sense of loss. *Must he stand so close? So wretchedly near and yet completely out of reach.*

He gibed her. "Another of your bracing morning walks, I take it?"

She refused to take the bait and glanced over her shoulder toward the old keep. "I had thought I might climb up to the ruins. But I . . ."

"Got waylaid by the brook."

"So it would seem."

"Catching trout with your toes?" He ran his finger along the arch of her foot, sending a burst of sensation up into her belly and an embarrassing heat into her cheeks.

She tucked her feet up under the hem of her gown. "I saw a few, but I'm afraid they were far too swift for my toes."

"Very wily trout in this brook. I used to fish at this very spot when I was a boy." A lock of his hair had fallen loose and hung by his cheek, shining like amber in the sunlight. *You ought not look at him.*

She pressed her fingers against the granite, letting the tiny little protrusions in the stone distract her senses. "It must have been wonderful growing up in a place so beautiful as this."

He glanced off into the distance and frowned. "It was quiet."

"No brothers or sisters to make noise?"

He sat down on the rock beside her, propping his boot against the rough surface and crossed his arms, still holding the reins. "I didn't realize you were a musician."

"I expect there are a great many things you do not know about me, my lord. But you have not answered my question."

"No. No brothers. No sisters."

"A pity. The manor is so large. I can almost imagine the stone walls echoing with the sound of children playing at sword fights and hide and seek."

"You have a vivid imagination. Aside from that, I did not live in the manor until I was much older."

"Oh? In St. Cleve, then?"

"Hardly." He chuckled, but not happily, almost as though she had made an annoying comment. "St. Cleve is, as you observed before, a lesser title. My grandfather portioned off the estate and sold it to local farmers. There remains a small independent village, the title, and a very meager income from one small farm. Nothing so generous as the thousand or two you had speculated on, my dear lady."

Elizabeth said nothing, but stared down at her hands folded in her lap. He had nothing in pocket. Which meant, of course, an alliance between them was impossible. She held back the telling sigh that fought to escape her throat. She would not think of it.

Valen slapped the ends of his reins against his other hand. "The scoundrel did it to ensure my father would have no money of his own." Pushing off the rock, he turned and planted his hands on either side of her, trapping her, staring straight into her eyes as if she were responsible for the acts of his grandfather. "You see, my father did a foolish thing in his youth—he fell in love."

She waited, her pulse throbbing mercilessly while he stood so close to her. She wanted to touch his cheek, pull his mouth to hers, soothe away his anger. But that would be unwise. *Ladies must not be forward. They must not lose their heads.* Her mind flapped around like a trapped wild bird, squawking inanities, *or else you will end up like Marie Antoinette, broken-hearted and headless. Too late. I might as well let them lop mine off right now. I am done for. In an instant and a half, if he doesn't move away, I will throw my arms around his neck, the consequences be damned.*

He studied her. "I'm not like you."

She swallowed. *No, thank the good Lord.* He was exceedingly different, gloriously male. And she adored every speck of that difference. The square hard lines of his face, the low rumble of his voice, the muscles of his shoulders—

"Shall I show you?"

She swallowed hard and nodded, uncertain as to what she was agreeing upon, but just now, he might ask her anything and she would give consent. Where was her father with his birch rod? Years of tutors and governesses, countless whippings and scoldings, and still, she hadn't learned a thing. She was still quite willing to take a flying leap off the roof—again.

"Then come." He lifted her up and set her on his horse.

This wasn't exactly what she expected.

He climbed up behind her, holding her as he urged his stallion forward.

"Where are we going?" Her question sounded ridiculously high and squeaky.

"To my real home."

"Now?"

"Yes."

"But my shoes."

He wheeled the horse and they crossed the creek to collect her stockings and shoes. He handed them up to her. As they rode off across the pasture, the only thing Elizabeth could think about was the feel of his arm pressing her against his chest and the

comforting reverberations of his voice as he intro-
duced her to Hercules, his horse, and as he re-
marked on each of the fields, their use, and his
plans for idle sections.

Less than half an hour later, they splashed across
another stream and headed around a hill into a
small vale. A rambling rose hedge served as a fence
for an ancient wattle and daub cottage. Their presence caused a stir.

"Papa! Papa!" A young boy dashed across the
yard toward the open front door, causing a con-
gregation of hens to cackle and flutter their wings.
"Valen's come home! He's here! An' he brought a
lady with him."

Elizabeth reached up to tuck back her hair. She
probably didn't look like much of a lady, with a
mud splattered walking dress and no shoes or
stockings.

A big man with the same fiery gold hair as Valen's
stepped quickly out of the door. "So it is! Meagan!
Pater! It's Valen!" he shouted back through the door
before approaching them with a hearty smile.

Before dismounting, Valen whispered beside
her ear, "This is my true home."

"How are you, my boy?" the big man asked as he
strode down the path.

Valen lifted Elizabeth to the ground and turned
to greet the farmer. They clapped hands and slapped
each other on the shoulder, staring with undisguised
joy at one another. "Thomas." Valen nodded.

Elizabeth suppressed a twinge of envy. *What must
I do to have him look upon me that way?*

Their reunion was interrupted by a scream
from the door and a woman rushing toward them
with a spoon in one hand and a kitchen rag in the
other. "Valentine!"

"Aunt Meg!" Valen greeted her with an embrace and the woman pelted his cheek with kisses. "Ach! But where are my manners? You've brought a young lady with you."

He presented her to his aunt and uncle, who bowed and curtseyed as if she were the mistress come to look over the servants. Elizabeth felt horribly awkward and couldn't think of what she might say to put them at ease.

Valen frowned.

"I'll see to your horse, shall I?" Farmer Thomas escaped the awkward moment by taking Hercules by the halter and pulling him toward a barn.

Meagan adjusted her apron and nudged Valen. "Bless me, but it is good to see you again. Have you had your breakfast? Why, of course, you haven't. Come in. Come in. It's just porridge and eggs, but it fills the empty places. Why, look at that—" She pointed her spoon at Elizabeth's naked feet. "Valen you'll have to carry her across the yard."

She waved the towel at the red and white feathered troop gathering behind her. "These chickens have been running loose all spring. Wouldn't want smush ending up between her toes, now would we? Come along. Pater has just sat down to bless the food."

Meagan shook her magic spoon toward the hedge. "Davy, my boy, that means you, too. We won't be waiting on you any longer. That cat can fend for itself."

"Yes, mum." The brown-haired lad, who had first alerted everyone to their presence, ducked his head from behind the rose bushes. Meagan prodded him toward the door with the spoon.

Valen turned to Elizabeth. "Well, Miss Shoeless,

I have been ordered to carry you past the chickens."

"I should think you would be heartily sick of lugging me around like a sack of potatoes."

"Always willing to be of service, my lady." He bowed, making a flourish of it, giving her an overdone show of obsequiousness.

She frowned at him. "Stop."

"I thought you enjoyed that sort of thing." He reached for her as if he intended to do precisely as she had said, and sling her over his shoulder like a bag of vegetables.

Elizabeth held up her hand and backed up, checking where she stepped. "If you will simply lend me your support and avert your eyes, I would prefer to put on my shoes and stockings."

"You may dress in peace, my lady." He inclined his head. "Your ankles are safe from my roaming eyes."

His sarcastic disinterest disappointed Elizabeth. He might, at least, have the decency to try and peek? To this end, she intentionally extended her leg out farther than necessary, while pulling on her stocking. She peeked sideways up at him to see if he'd noticed and grimaced when she spied his arched brow. It wasn't arched as if he were pleasantly surprised. No. Not he. He wore a condemning sneer.

"Tch tch, Izzie, machinating again? Another ploy like that, my dear, and I will let go of you. In which case, you will have a choice of falling against that thorny rose bush or onto this path littered with fresh chicken excrement."

"I most certainly am not machinating."

"You were."

"You wouldn't let me fall, surely?" She had no doubt he *would* drop her. The roses sported some savage looking thorns and the excrement held very little appeal. Elizabeth bent to her task with more diligence. "Wretch," she mumbled.

"Merely being practical. I would not want to fall prey to the shapeliness of your ankle. I've heard men rhapsodize about the fatality of such things. The medusa effect and all."

"I sincerely doubt you are capable of falling prey to anyone, my lord," she muttered as they walked into the house. "Not even Medusa." After all, Medusa could hardly turn him into stone. He already appeared to be made of the stuff.

Valen led her to a low-ceilinged room with heavy beams. There were so many bundles of herbs tacked up on the beams for drying that Elizabeth had to dodge them as she entered the dining room. At the head of a long worn board table sat a willowy gentleman with snowy white hair. He stood up, stooping to avoid wearing a face full of drying blackberry leaves.

"My grandfather, Benjamin Whitley, Steward of Ransley Keep." Valen's voice was proud and held a note of awe.

Elizabeth could see why. The older man's wizened expression made her think he could see straight into her soul. She swallowed.

Meagan directed Elizabeth to a seat next to a gangly young man of about five and ten years, who blushed when she sat down. Valen took his place beside his grandfather. He and Valen exchanged knowing looks, understanding running openly between them.

Five children and as many adults gathered around the table and between them all they devoured a huge pot of porridge, a crockery bowl full of eggs, a pan of stewed pears, and two pitchers of fresh milk. Although, one sneaky kitten, who roamed among the children, assisted them, inducing them to spill a small portion of their milk. This, the children willingly did every time Meagan turned her back.

After Thomas excused himself to tend to chores and took most of the boys with him, Meagan hefted an empty pitcher and turned to her youngest. "David Whitley, you've been feeding that cat again, haven't you?" He nodded remorsefully, grinned and scampered off before he could receive a proper scold. Elizabeth laughed and asked how she might help clean up.

"Oh no, couldn't do that," Meagan protested. "Wouldn't be right. You're our guest, and a lady."

"I daresay, I'm an intruder you were gracious enough to feed. However, I will strike you a bargain." She lifted a handful of the red clover heads from her pocket. "Perhaps, if I help you in the kitchen, you would be willing to tell me the best way to dry these so I might make a tea for Lord Ransley."

"He's worse then, is he?" Meagan sighed as she carried an armful of plates and bowls to the kitchen. Elizabeth and one of the girls followed suit.

Meagan wiped her hand on a towel she kept tucked into her skirt. "Pater visits him once a week now that he's been reinstated as steward. He mentioned as how Lord Ransley's lungs were failing, but men don't pay heed to the details. It's bad then, is it?"

"He does not appear well at all. Labors to speak. His skin is pale and . . ." Elizabeth answered softly, hoping Valen did not hear. But, even as he spoke to his grandfather in the other room, he watched her. She lowered her voice to a whisper. "There is some blood when he coughs. Surely, there are some herbs that might ease his condition? I found an old book of remedies in our attic at home. Unfortunately, I don't have it with me. And I'm uncertain which ones—"

"Come," Meagan beckoned. "My daughter will tend to these. Come with me to the garden."

Meagan's garden stretched along the entire length of the back of the cottage. There were flowers everywhere, hollyhocks and raspberries in bloom, new vegetable growth in neatly tended rows, and patches of medicinal herbs scattered among the blossoms.

"You'll want mallow, grows by the pond." Meagan led her around a little stone path that weaved in and among all the plants. "I've got a firkin of dried cherry bark inside, you can brew some of that in a tea for his cough, and add licorice to calm the spasms. You were right about the clover, but be cautious. If it doesn't soothe him straight off, take it away. Try the roots of this, after they're dried. Grind them and make powder." She handed her an odd looking plant with stringy leaves and gray roots. "Has Valentine told you about his mother yet?"

The non sequitur surprised Elizabeth. They stood among the giant round blossoms of alum and garlic, facing each other. Meagan was a plain guileless woman, with strong bones and features that would not be able to dissemble should she attempt it for a hundred years. And she expected an answer.

"No. Only that his father fell in love. And the previous Lord Ransley made things difficult."

Meagan nodded. "That he did. Made them both suffer for it. Then when Valentine was born . . .

Well, more's the pity. I think he paid the highest price of all. It's not my place to say more. Surely, he'll tell you in good time. But, oh, I wish you could have known his mother."

Meagan glanced away as if seeing faces from another era. "She was not more than twelve when I married Thomas and came to live here. A rare one, she was. So bright and lively. So in love with young Ransley. It's no wonder they ran off to Gretna Green." She slapped her hands against her thighs. "There now, I've said too much."

Meg bent and pulled up an allium. "Here's garlic. Make a paste with butter and spread it on his toast. Strengthens the blood."

Valen stood at the window beside his grandfather.

Pater slapped him on the shoulder. "She's a fine-looking woman."

"Too haughty by half." He watched Meagan stack a bouquet of garlic into Elizabeth's arms. The long stalks had white flowers that brushed against Izzie's chin. She tried to adjust the plants, but only succeeded in shifting the blossoms so they brushed against her nose. She sneezed.

"Doesn't look haughty at the moment." His grandfather observed.

"No, but put her in a ballroom and she has enough arrogance to float an armada."

"And, of course, you have none."

He frowned. "I am not arrogant."

"No, of course not."

Valen could tell by the crinkled corner of Pater's mouth that he believed he was.

"You know perfectly well that I despise arrogance. And you know the reason why."

"Yes." Pater nodded. "You hate it so much that you run the risk of being proud about not being proud."

"You're speaking in circles." Valen shrugged and turned back to the window. Elizabeth had dropped her load and was bent over picking up garlic and a host of other green things.

"Is that what they taught you at college?" His grandfather chuckled. "Avoid the truth by arguing about the form of the argument."

Izzie swatted at a flying insect and danced sideways to avoid its counterattack.

"Could be you don't see her correctly." Pater chuckled at her antics. "The woman heats your blood. I can see it in your eyes."

He had never discussed such things with his grandfather. Everything else under the sun, but not this. Valen shifted uncomfortably. "There are far more important things than hot blood."

Pater sighed deeply. "Undoubtedly. But I wonder, Valen, is a man's fire kindled before, or after, he observes the character traits of the woman?"

Her traits. Oh yes, aside from the haughtiness, she was headstrong, devious, and had a viperous tongue. Exactly when did he first develop this irritating attraction to Lady Elizabeth? He couldn't recall. All too soon in their acquaintance. It certainly wasn't owing to her fine character.

His grandfather paused, giving him time to answer, but when Valen failed to respond, he argued on without him. "It could be, your body is telling you something your mind is hardened against hearing. Have you considered that?"

"An unorthodox notion, Pater." Valen folded his arms across his chest and broadened his stance. "Unfortunately, it's flawed. My stallion heats up over any eligible mare within a ten-mile radius, regardless of her characteristics. I daresay, even if it were a broken-down donkey he would be quite content to roger her."

"And you, Valen? Are you like your stallion? Do you heat up over every female within a ten-mile radius?" His grandfather turned on him, spearing Valen's defenses with that knowing stare that always pierced him to the marrow. "There are some unscrupulous men who do, but I cannot for one minute believe you are one of them."

Valen took a deep breath and turned back to the window to watch Lady Elizabeth Hampton, the daughter of an earl, walk side by side through the garden with Meg, the daughter of a Harwich fisherman.

Chapter 17

Unraveling a Tightly Knit Paradox

The sun passed its zenith before they set out on Hercules, riding back to Ransley Keep. She sat silent, clutching a bag of herbs, and he held her in place with a hand on her belly and an ache in regions he did not wish to acknowledge. His grandfather's words kept marching in circles in his head. Was his randy body telling him something his mind simply refused to hear? Devil take it! He would prove it wasn't so.

"So, now you know." The declaration burst out of him like a challenge.

She tilted her head, tickling his chin with flighty strands of silky black hair. "What is it I know?"

"My birthright. Half blood." He spat it out in curt businesslike snippets. "Father an aristocrat. Mother common."

"I don't see that it is of much consequence. Your father is a nobleman. That makes you a nobleman." She shifted the bag of herbs, holding it a little tighter. "Does it trouble you?"

"Only the noble half."

She turned to look up at him. "You would rather—"

"I'd trade with Thomas in a trice." He averted his eyes from her face. He would not look at that mouth of hers, wouldn't allow his gaze to linger on the inviting curve of her cheek, refused to meet her disturbingly blue eyes.

"Oh." She turned away, fiddling with the drawstrings on the burlap bag. "Well, I can certainly see why. They're very happy."

"That's not the reason." He practically growled it. "I detest the Ransley blood. The sixth Lord of Ransley . . ." He struggled to bite back his rising fury. ". . . was an arrogant prig. And my father was too weak to stand up to him."

"And yet, he had the courage to marry your mother—against the former lord's wishes, I assume."

"Apparently that was as far as his fortitude extended. He stood by, allowing my mother to be belittled severely. She left the manor and went home to live with Pater and my uncle. They both believed the old man would soften after I was born. To the contrary, he fought even harder to have the marriage annulled and me declared a bastard— my common blood insulted the Ransley name. I wish he'd succeeded. On that one point, my father prevailed. But the old goat kept them apart. My mother died a year before he did."

"And because of this one man you would deny your heritage? Your birthright?"

"Heritage? Birthright? Spoken like a true aristocrat." *There! Pater is wrong. Aristocracy is more impor-*

tant to her than the lives of two people. His triumph felt oddly flat, like discovering the rose does have razor sharp thorns. He'd expected it. Nevertheless, it disappointed him to cut his fingers. "The whole pompous notion of nobility is absurd. What makes a man more noble than another? The accident of his birth? The world would have been better off had the sixth Lord of Ransley been born a swineherd. Even then, I suspect he would have made the pigs miserable. If he ever nurtured a noble impulse in his entire life, it is news to me. Whereas, Pater—"

"I grasp your point," she answered dully.

And she did. All too well. Elizabeth understood with perfect clarity why Valen disliked her so thoroughly. She stood no chance of winning his admiration because of the accident of *her* birth. She clasped the herb bag firmly in her lap, absently squeezing at one of the garlic bulbs until she felt the pressure nearly burst the cloves apart.

"Well, at least, now, I comprehend Miss Dunworthy's appeal." Her remark tripped out sounding horridly spiteful. But Elizabeth couldn't stop her runaway tongue. "The dear girl is possessed of both money and a common birth. You must be in alt." As soon as she said it, she wished she could bite back the hasty words—they stunk of such sour grapes. But what did it matter? His high and mighty lordship preferred mushrooms to ladies of quality. He left her no fair ground on which to compete.

"Exactly," he said, with such consummate arrogance she dearly wished to slap him. "You've proven my point. You think you are better than Miss Dunworthy, simply because she hasn't a pedigree that compares to yours."

"Kindly set me down here, my lord." Elizabeth emphasized the "my lord" and pointed emphatically at the ground below them.

Rather than complying, he tightened his hold around her middle.

Insolent man. "I should prefer to walk."

"I think not."

She simmered for a moment before thinking of the perfect rejoinder. "Pray, tell me this, Lord St. Cleve. When your son is born, will you despise him because he is noble?"

Valen stiffened. *A son?* The image of an infant, his son, shot into his mind, nearly knocking him off his horse. He tried to shake it away. She ought not speak of babes when he had his hand on her abdomen and a very informative view of her breasts every time he glanced down. All too easy to imagine her swollen with his child. The ache in his witless body mounted unbearably.

He must be one of those men Pater mentioned—as randy as his unprincipled stallion. He ought to set her down, right here, right now, in the middle of this field, ride away and not look back. She was precisely the sort of female he wished to avoid.

She prattled at him, ". . . a perfectly respectful request. The least you could do, as a gentleman, is honor it and put me down this instant. I have no wish to travel further with you in the intimate confines of this horse—"

"Intimate confines?" He laughed. "We're on horseback in the middle of the open countryside. There are any number of shepherds acting as chaperone. Not to mention Aunt Honore is probably in one of the upstairs windows, this very minute, with a spy-glass trained on us. Hardly intimate."

She glanced nervously in the direction of the manor. "Be that as it may, you have expressed such a strong aversion to my character that rather than annoy you with my presence I would rather—"

She did annoy him, far more than she realized. "I have a better idea." He gripped her tighter and wheeled Hercules. The sudden movement jarred Izzie. She nearly let go of the sack, hanging onto it with one hand and clutching his thigh in a frantic attempt to steady herself. He laughed again, out of sheer orneriness, and let the stallion run.

"What in heavens name—" She gripped his leg tighter as they galloped toward the hill. When they jumped a low rock border, she yelped. His bother-some conscience chided him for frightening her. He slowed the pace. They were climbing the hill anyway.

Once she caught her breath, she started in on him. "I demand you—"

"You said you wished to see the old ruins. I am simply doing my duty as an obliging host."

She tentatively let go of his leg, dusting her hand off on her skirt. "You might have mentioned. It is customary to give a person warning before—"

"Lady Elizabeth, do you ever cease scolding?"

She fell silent as they climbed the hill. One would think he would enjoy a reprieve from her tongue, but Valen found the silence irritating. He would much rather know what she was thinking—thorns and all.

Much of the stone from the old keep had been carted away to build the new manor, or tenant's

huts, sheep holds, or field borders. All that remained was a collapsing maze of walls, most of
which were no taller than Valen's shoulder. It was a
maze he knew well. A place he had played as a boy,
where he alone reigned king, and banished evil
men like the sixth Lord of Ransley to the dungeon.

Valen left Hercules to graze amongst the scattered stones and led Elizabeth through the crumbling castle to the eastern curtain wall. He hoisted
himself up onto the thick ledge and gazed out
over the vista. "Come up. From here you can almost see the channel."

She glanced skeptically at the worn stone ridge
and muttered, "Ladies do not climb . . ."

He couldn't hear the rest. "Are you not the lass
who spread her wings from the roof? Come. At the
highest point, it is only five or six feet off the
ground. Never mind, I'll come and help you." A
fatal mistake.

Valen leaped down, lifted her up onto a lower
section, and then jumped up onto the wall beside
her. Holding Elizabeth's hand, they tread carefully
across the precipice. She hesitated before every
step, testing each stone for stability; her arm, stiff
and tense, shook as she climbed higher.

"You're trembling?" It surprised him that she of
all people should find this difficult.

Her gaze flitted briefly from the ground to his
face. "Ever since that day . . ."

"Ah." He nodded. "Then I won't press you to go
any further." He steadied her, wrapping his arm
around her waist. "If you can, look out at the horizon. There." He pointed east, in the direction of
the sea.

The land sloped in series of swells and tables

until, many miles away, it met the water. He loved this place. Staring for hours at that distant invisible sea when he was young, dreaming of the day he would sail away to the exotic places that water might carry him, places far away from the suffering of his parents.

"Perhaps, if we sit, you will stop quaking."

"I am not quaking." Her relentless pride in the face of the obvious was a marvel.

"No, of course not. Begging your pardon, I am the one nearly shaking the wall apart."

"Very well, then. For your sake, I will sit." She cautiously eased down onto the wall and seemed to breathe easier once she situated herself.

They dangled their legs over the precipice, gazing out over the lands below. She relaxed enough that he even saw her foot bounce contently.

"I must go back tomorrow." He didn't know why he brought it up now. But he wanted to make sure she knew he would be leaving her soon.

She lowered her gaze, studying the ground beneath them again, the little bounce in her foot stilled. "I thought you might."

He had the ridiculous urge to gather her in his arms and reassure her. Naturally, he didn't succumb. "You will be safe here with my father. Perhaps you might do him some good."

"It is my hope."

He disliked hearing the bravado in her voice, the stalwart, chin-up tone he had come to recognize in her. He ignored it. "He will do well with your company."

She left off searching the horizon and turned to him, suddenly earnest. "Promise you will be cautious hunting Merót?" She placed her hand on the stone beside his, her fingers resting on his thumb. "Promise."

He couldn't ignore the pleading in her expression. The randy stallion inside him sniffed the air. God help him, she had some sort of bewitching power over him. One miniscule touch, one caring glance . . . He tried to make light of her concern. "I am always cautious."

A bold-faced lie. Rash, came more readily to mind. After all, if he were the cautious sort he wouldn't be sitting here atop an old ruin, alone with a woman who made his blood pound like war drums through his veins.

The stallion in him pawed at the ground, straining at the bit. What harm would there be if he kissed her? What harm, indeed? He could think of a hundred reasons why it would be a reckless, foolhardy, and an altogether stupid thing to do. Still, he would leave tomorrow and wouldn't see her for who knows how long . . .

He growled low in his throat. Valen had no patience for long internal debates. He thrust the question into her hands. "I wish to kiss you."

She put a hand to her breast and shook her head. "You are asking? How very out of character."

What sort of reply was that? A challenge? A diversion? An evasive tactic? She would not escape so easily.

"And you, Elizabeth?" He didn't touch her. Didn't lean toward her mouth, but he did slowly peruse her lips. "Do you wish it?"

"I confess, I do not understand you, my lord." She drew back, flustered, bristling. "One minute, with no little heat I might add, you tell me that I am the antithesis of all you hold dear. And now?

Now, you ask me if I wish to . . ." She stopped abruptly, and stared at his mouth. Contemplating, he judged. "It is most confusing."

"Hmm. Yes. It's the wretched heat." He allowed one side of his mouth to curl up in a sardonic grin. "Well, do you?"

"Do I what?" She cringed.

"You know perfectly well. Do you wish to kiss me?"

"The question itself is preposterous. After all your gibes, the insults, and lectures on the ignobility of my nobility—"

"Answer the question, Lady Elizabeth. Do you want me to?"

"I don't see that it matters."

"Answer."

"Why? So that you may chide me? Tell me what a poor example of virtue I am?"

"No. So that I may kiss you."

"Do you mean to say, you won't, if I say nay?"

"I make no promises."

The breeze carried fine black strands of her hair and wrapped them around her cheek. Valen tucked them back behind her ear, gliding his fingertips across the smooth crest of her cheek. "Do you?" he whispered. Now he needed the answer as much as he needed to breathe. *She has to want me. Has to! I cannot be the only one.*

When she met his gaze, he had his answer. Clear blue eyes had never looked so hungry.

Nor so sweet.

Nor so innocent.

Or perplexed.

He groaned. Devil take it! He couldn't make her answer now. He would hate himself for putting her to the test. Aside from that, the heat he had known before now seemed insignificant. That one small glance from her had jolted through him like a static charge, igniting fires he didn't know existed.

"You need not answer." Valen swore under his breath. *Reckless.* Now he was the one confused. "It was a foolish question. I will take you back to the manor now."

He jumped down from the wall and held out his arms to her. Elizabeth slid trustingly from the wall into his embrace. She didn't leave her hands on his shoulders. Instead, she entwined them around his neck, resting her body against his, and whispered huskily in his ear, "Yes."

Then she sought his lips, and he thought perhaps heaven had descended upon him, so sweet was her kiss.

He had no defense. The power of it all overwhelmed him. Never in his life had he wanted anything, or anyone, so much as he wanted her in that moment. At the same time, never had he been so willing to deny himself.

What was happening to him? Perhaps, he had fallen ill and this was all a feverish delirium.

If she didn't stop kissing him soon, it would be too late. The flimsy inkling of restraint he had left would dissolve.

Wild, untamed thoughts galloped through his head. Dizzy, breathing as if he'd just run down the hill and back again, Valen took her face in his hands. "Izzie, my sweet, there is not another woman in heaven or earth I would rather kiss. But if we do not leave now . . . well, then I cannot account for my lusty stallion."

She blinked, failing to grasp his inanity. He grimaced, praying he wouldn't have to explain.

"Oh." Comprehension dawned in her pure blue eyes. "You're worried about your horse running off."

He tried not to let the corner of his mouth twitch. "Yes. That's it."

Her innocent disappointment tweaked his conscience, but he decided they would both fare better if he left the matter unexplained.

He lifted her onto Hercules's back and held the reins, walking alongside them back to Ransley Keep. He couldn't ride behind her, holding her as he had. Her scent alone would drive him to madness. So, for the sake of his sanity, and her virtue, they had a long quiet stroll back to the manor. During which time, Valen pondered the complexity of a God who would create such an ironic paradox as to make him fall in love with a woman he could scarcely tolerate, but did not want to live without.

Chapter 18

Whatsoever Ye Sew, So Shall Ye Wear

"Remarkable."

"Yes, m'lord. The first time since Christmas, I believe."

"You're right." Valen rubbed his chin. "Are you certain he's well enough?"

"It isn't for me to say, m'lord. He wishes it." The butler inclined his head and backed away.

Elizabeth and Valen had been greeted with the news that Lord Ransley intended to take his evening meal with all of them in the dining room and that he had even arranged for entertainment afterward.

As they had journeyed back to the keep, Elizabeth had grown steadily more and more vexed. Evidently, she brooded, her kisses had so little effect on Lord St. Cleve that he preferred to attend to the welfare of his horse—a humiliating revelation. One, which made Elizabeth question whether she had any power over men at all.

"And shall we dress?" she asked peevishly. "Or will you be appearing in your shirtsleeves?"

"I suppose that depends on whether the servants have been able to scrub your slobber out from my dress shirt."

Callous of him to remind her of that, but, oh, so very typical. Well, he needn't have bothered. She refused to allow him to discomfit her any further. "I'm certain you must have others."

"I might. But I liked that one."

Relentless goad. She elevated her chin and shrugged. "You may wear whatever you choose. It makes absolutely no difference to me."

"Absolutely none?" He bowed. "Why, thank you, your majesty. Your forbearance is a marvel."

Would that he thought her beauty was a marvel, but, of course, he had proved immune to any of that sort of thing. He preferred to tease her and test her. Well, she'd had enough. "Kindly direct me to the kitchen." She needed to put the herbs into storage.

"The kitchen?" He feigned shock. "Oh, but surely a great lady such as yourself ought not—"

"Very well." She shoved the bag of garlic and various other pungent plants at her court jester. "You take them and see that you put them away properly."

He straightened and refused to take the bag from her, quirking up one side of his cheek. "Down the rear stairwell, turn left, and you will undoubtedly collide with several members of the kitchen staff—all anxious to do your bidding."

"Thank you." She spun on her heel and walked away from him making certain she did not sway her hips. Such a thing would be wasted on him.

Well . . . perhaps a little sway in your walk is perfectly natural, as long as you do it gracefully. She glanced back over her shoulder and was rewarded with his wickedly mocking grin.

Later, in the privacy of her room she sorted through her gowns, and laid out three on her bed. Which one was most suitable for a viscount's table? Which was her most attractive? It ought not to be a difficult decision given the fact that there were only three suitable gowns, and one Valen had already seen. Indeed, he had a coat that matched it superbly. Well, perhaps "superb" wasn't an apt description. And, in actuality, he no longer had the coat, she did. Nevertheless, the point stood. That particular gown was out.

Servants entered, carrying a luxurious copper tub, and filled it with buckets of inviting warm water. As soon as they left, Elizabeth disrobed and stepped in, gliding comfortably into the heavenly warmth, sinking up to her chin. She rinsed off the grime of the past two days, and then lolled her head back to rest. As her muscles began to loosen, she glanced over to the bed and considered the gowns.

Glittering gold silk or plain iced purple? Don't be silly. What does it matter? It's a simple family dinner, not a London ball. Aside from that, who did she seek to impress? Certainly not him. Not Valen. Heavens no!

Not only was he a rascal bent on bedeviling her at every turn, but also, he probably hadn't enough money to pay off her father's old tailoring bill much less set her younger sisters up for a Season, or to have the roof mended. The farrier, some servants and a few others, had been compensated by the sale of their livestock. Even so, there remained a heavy stack of bills yet to meet, and she sincerely doubted Lord St. Insulting had a large enough allowance to cover it.

That settled the matter. She was a pauper, and so she would dress humbly, in the simple purple silk. She closed her eyes and leaned back in the tub, commanding herself to relax. It felt delicious to bathe after such a tedious morning. Tedious, yes, that was it. Tedious, to have his arms around her. Tedious, to be kissed in such a manner. Of course, in truth, she had kissed him. Elizabeth opened her eyes and frowned, unable to relax any longer.

"The wretch." She slapped at the bathwater, sending a spray splashing out onto the stone floor.

They gathered in the great hall. Servants carried Lord Ransley down in an invalid's chair and wheeled him into their midst. His brown wispy hair was coifed perfectly and, if one overlooked the white cast of his complexion, he looked quite elegant in a blue superfine coat.

Elizabeth curtseyed.

He waved her up. "And my son? I thought surely he would be down before me."

"Better not have gone off riding again," Lady Alameda warned the absent Valen with considerable irritation. "I'll ring a bell over his head he won't soon forget."

"Peal," Elizabeth murmured.

"Precisely. I'll peel back his ears." But before the countess need peel or pin anyone's ears, Valen descended the stairs.

Elizabeth's heart thumped up into her neck.

His hair had been cut short. He wore a waistcoat made of a subtle gold brocade and his black cut-away was tailored so exquisitely that every Corinthian in London would be envious. Elizabeth remembered to breathe at the same time she realized she'd se-lected the wrong dress. She would appear a simple country mouse, and he a sophisticated paragon.

"What are you all staring at?" He arched one brow as he strolled up to them and all three continued gawking as if he were an apparition.

Elizabeth felt like she ought to curtsey. Instead, she dropped onto a chair and frowned down at her icy purple gown with its prudent neckline and plain lines.

"You scrub up rather well, dearest." Lady Alameda kissed Valen on the cheek.

"Yes." Lord Ransley coughed. "Don't believe I've ever seen you—"

"You may thank your valet. Merely a haircut. One would think I sprouted horns."

The valet peeked out at the top of the stairs, peering proudly at his handiwork.

Valen rolled his eyes heavenward. "You may all congratulate him later. Are we going to go into dinner, or not? If we intend to follow the formalities, my lord, I believe you and my aunt are supposed to lead the way."

He held out his arm for Elizabeth, but as soon as she accepted and rose to her feet, he assumed the position of pushing his father's chair. Lady Alameda walked beside her brother and Elizabeth walked next to Valen in stunned silence.

The dining room walls were a series of inset wooden panels. Each of the panels were outlined in carved casings and set in the middle with a pastoral scene, or a painting of a royal hunting party, dogs, roosters, or great bowls of flowers. At the far end of the room, stood a gigantic carved fireplace, unlit because of the warmth of the evening. With the dark walls, even the giant candelabras were able to do little to illuminate the room.

The table was arranged *en famille,* so that they all sat together at one end of the massive table, while servants silently laid out the first course. Lord Ransley coughed into his handkerchief, but when he recovered, he looked out at his guests in pleasure.

Valen frowned. "Are you absolutely certain the exertion is not too—"

Lord Ransley waved away his son's concerns. "No. No. This is the happiest day I've had in a long while." He nodded and smiled broadly. "Feeling quite the thing today. Had the windows open. Perhaps, the fresh air did me some good."

Honore dipped up her white soup, and sipped it loudly as was the custom. "Did you enjoy your tour of the ruins today, Lady Elizabeth?"

"Yes." Elizabeth glanced guiltily at Valen. "I . . . They were very . . . uh . . . interesting."

"I warned you." Valen shrugged. "Telescope at the upstairs window, no doubt."

Lady Alameda appeared affronted. "Whatever can you mean?"

Valen didn't answer, merely cocked his head and smiled sardonically at his aunt.

Lady Alameda concentrated on her soup, scooping up a spoonful laden with almonds. "We were simply concerned about where Lady Elizabeth might have gotten off to, what with spies running about the countryside and all."

Valen shook his head at them as if they were a pair of wayward children. "I think it is safe to say the only spies up here in Suffolk are you two."

"You were both at the window?" Elizabeth murmured, wishing she might crawl under the table and hide.

"Piffle. We weren't spying. I was merely showing your father the new glass I'd purchased. Latest rage. Everyone has one. Daresay, mine is considerably more advanced than the ones most sea captains have."

"I've no doubt." Valen seemed unconcerned that he and Elizabeth had been watched, their private moments invaded.

Exactly how much had they seen? Elizabeth worried. Had they witnessed her brazenly throwing herself into his embrace?

"Purely an accident we happened to sight you two at the old castle. Now, let me see, what were we discussing . . ." Lady Alameda tapped her spoon against the tablecloth. "Oh yes, I don't believe you answered my question, Lady Elizabeth. Did you enjoy yourself?"

Lord Ransley coughed and frowned heavily at his sister over the edge of his kerchief. "Second course already, Honore, and you've hardly touched your soup."

The countess lifted another spoonful, a piece of thinly sliced bacon dripping over the edge, and mumbled, "Hmm. Well, it certainly looked to me as if she were enjoying herself." She slurped loudly.

Lord Ransley shook his head.

Elizabeth's cheeks flamed up, and her own soup spoon wobbled horridly as she attempted to carry it to her mouth. A slice of celery dropped to the table.

Chapter 19

Silver Threads of Moonlight and Muddles

The remainder of dinner passed in relative silence apart from Lord Ransley's coughing spasms. As they finished up over quince tarts and Stilton cheese, he announced that he had hired some local musicians to entertain them for the evening.

Lady Alameda grumbled. "It's those odd Evermeyer sisters and their old-maid aunt. Whoever heard of three spinsters serving as musicians? Out of the ordinary way, if anyone were to ask me."

"High praise, indeed, coming from you." Valen rolled his father's chair out of the dining room and down the hallway. "A lady well known for orchestrating a wide variety of mischief."

"Mischief? Fiddle-faddle. Stand aside, I'll do this." She nudged Valen out of the way and took over pushing Lord Ransley. "Mischievous. Me? Ha. You are all about in your head, my boy. Obviously, you've had too much wine with dinner." Putting her back into the task, she shoved her brother vigorously ahead of Valen into the gallery.

"She saw everything," Elizabeth whispered to him.

"Can you doubt it?"

No, but I was hoping.

Valen chuckled, obviously not as disconcerted as she, and led her into a long gallery whose doors hung open to the gardens in the back of the manor.

Three middle-aged women sprang to attention at their approach and curtseyed charmingly to Lord Ransley. He expressed his gratitude at their coming on such short notice and explained that he wished to take the evening air, stroll about the garden, while they played. "Your excellent music will make the evening perfect."

The three musicians took their place at their instruments—the piano, a harp, and a flute.

Before they went out through the large double doors, Lady Alameda turned to Elizabeth and whispered behind her fan, "Perhaps you might like to perform with them, Lady Elizabeth? You play the recorder, do you not?"

Elizabeth endeavored to smile. "Perhaps the sound did not carry well enough across the fields, my lady. I am certainly not proficient enough to play for company."

"Ah, well, a pity. You would fit so well in their midst, don't you think?" She waved at the trio warming up their instruments.

Lady Alameda pushed her brother through the doors, leaving Elizabeth to puzzle out the meaning of her cryptic observation. Was it because her pastel gown would coordinate with the light shades of the fluttering pink and green gowns of the sisters?

Or was it because the countess considered her, like the musicians, a spinster?

Lord St. Cleve took Elizabeth's arm and they walked in the evening air, the scent of roses floated like twirling gauze on the breeze, brushing against their nostrils, while the piquant notes of Mozart's concerto danced around them like audible fireflies.

The manor gardens were fit for a royal palace, with huge ball and arrow topiaries that must have taken decades to shape, stone benches, and a fountain in the center. In the waning light Elizabeth could not identify the individual flowers, but she caught glimpses of their color patterns artistically arranged in neatly kept borders.

In short order, Lord Ransley's cough worsened. "Regrettably, I must retire for the evening." He had another fit and waved his hand at them. "But I insist you must stay, enjoy the music and air as long as you wish." As he continued to cough, Lady Alameda rolled him back to the house.

Elizabeth watched them go and couldn't help but feel she and Valen had been maneuvered into the situation. "Perhaps we ought to return as well."

Valen brushed a lacewing fly away from her hair. "It would be a pity to waste such a beautiful night, such a perfect setting. Indeed, I believe the two of them have gone to a great deal of trouble to make it nearly ideal."

Nearly? What could be lacking, she wondered, aside from the correct partner to share it with? "It is too bad Miss Dunworthy cannot be here to share it with you."

"Don't spoil it, Izzie." He took her hand and raised it to his lips. "Can you really be so blind?"

She said nothing, but watched him press a kiss on her fingers.

"Even my father is under the impression I feel passionately about you."

"You must enlighten him."

The corner of his mouth curled up. "And how would you suggest I do that?"

"Tell him the truth, that you dislike me excessively."

"The truth? Then I would have to explain to him that I wish to make love to you every time I see you." He set her hand, the one he had just kissed, on his forearm. "Did I mention that you look particularly bewitching tonight?"

"No." She stared at him, dazed.

"Well, you do." He smiled warmly. "I'd mistakenly thought your inventive gowns were partly to blame for my inability to resist you. Yet, tonight, when I saw you in this dress, which reveals nothing, and still I felt such an overwhelming—"

"Stop." She held up her hand. "Kindly repeat that part again."

"Which part?"

"The . . ." She bit the edge of her lip, unsure how to proceed without being indelicate. "The 'make love' part."

"Ah. You would triumph over me." He leaned his head back, staring at the sky as if the stars and the moon might explain the complexities of woman. "You would reduce a man to the sum of his urges. Very well, my lady, I will tell you. You drive me to madness for want of you." He frowned. "There. Does that please you?"

Elizabeth shook her head. *It could not be.* "It can't be. What of today? You stopped." She stamped her foot, slipper striking feebly against the gravel path. "Because of your *horse*."

"Ahh." He laughed at her.

She glowered at him and crossed her arms.

"And if I hadn't stopped?" He tilted his head toward her, his words husky and rich, thrumming harmoniously with the deep harp strains swirling around them.

She considered his question. *I should have enjoyed it very much.* But in the dim evening light, she noted the heat in his expression and realized her error. How very shortsighted she had been.

"Do you think I am made of stone?"

Yes. No. She stepped back and shook her head.

"Did you think I could withstand the onslaught of your kisses without being moved?"

She averted her eyes. "I did not intend . . ."

"No." He chucked her chin. "I don't believe you did. Come. Walk with me. Before I am forced to kiss you again, right here in my father's garden."

He secured her hand on his arm and leaned to her ear, whispering conspiratorially, "They are probably, this very minute, up there cracking open the window and extending the telescope, giggling like a couple of schoolgirls."

She ignored his aside, still struggling to comprehend his declaration. "I thought you merely enjoyed taunting me. I didn't believe you truly hid any warmth behind it."

"There is no accounting for it, I agree."

She squinted at the trees in the park ahead of them, and thought she saw something rustling the shrubbery—probably a fox or an owl. "But, we are not suited. You have said as much on several occasions."

"Exactly."

"You needn't agree so readily."

He patted her hand. "Would you have me deny the truth? That I find you arrogant in the extreme and—"

She yanked her hand away and turned to him, hands on hips. "I am not arrogant."

"You most certainly are. And you have the sharpest tongue in all of Christendom."

"I do not."

"Right." He knocked his palm against his forehead. "I forgot about my aunt. Very well, you have the second most lethal tongue."

"Flatterer." She crossed her arms.

He chuckled. "Yet, in the face of it all, I find I am completely done for."

"You have my sympathy."

"I'm serious, Izzie." He rubbed his hand against the satin on her shoulder. "What if I told you that I can no longer deny the passion I feel?"

He took his hand away from her shoulder.

She waited.

"It is unexplainable, this force within me. Nevertheless, I accept the reality of it. And after today, I cannot imagine . . ." He kneaded his brow for a moment and then straightened, soldierlike. "Life without you simply would not be palatable."

It sounded very nearly like a proposal, and yet he was not down on one knee, he had not ascribed her beauty, or her character, as the source of his passion. Nay, he had ranted about her reprehensible traits.

"I am not quite certain what you are asking, my lord. But I am very sorry for your palate—to have to deny it such a distasteful morsel."

He groaned. "You've taken offense."

"It surprises you? You tell me you think me a

perfectly dreadful person, and yet, much to your dismay, some wretched part of your physiology prefers to keep me nearby. I have no idea whether this is an indecent proposition, or a proposal."

He lifted a hand to heaven as if he might grab some help there. "It's glaringly obvious, Izzie. I'm asking you to marry me. I may have done it badly . . ."

She nodded enthusiastically.

He grasped her shoulders. "But surely you understand my bewilderment. You've held me in contempt since we first met. I felt certain you had as much aversion to me as I did to you. And then today . . . This is all very confusing."

"On that point, we are in agreement." She sniffed and refused to look at him, she might almost fall for that earnest expression in his eyes.

"Look at me, Izzie."

"No."

"Please."

She reluctantly complied.

"Things have changed." He said it with a sincerity that almost frightened her.

"Not all things." Elizabeth could not keep her chin from jutting up defensively. "You still insist on insulting me at every opportunity. And—"

"Is that it?" He squeezed her shoulders and let go. "You wish me to humble myself at your alter. Praise your beauty. Wax poetic over the softness of your lips. Tell you how I envy the moonlight because it touches your hair." He exhaled loudly. "I'm a man of action, Izzie. If I say such things aloud, I'm apt to yank out your pins and let your hair fall into my palm. Why talk about lips, when I might be tasting them?"

She stood there, wishing he would do exactly that. But he didn't. Instead he left her raw senses at the mercy of the caressing breeze and the seductive music.

Elizabeth sighed and sat down on a bench. Valen stood in front of her like a Viking warlord losing his patience.

She could not drum up a confident air. "You are right. This is all very confusing." In the face of her weakness and turmoil, her training reared its head. *I have obligations.*

She glanced up at Valen, knowing before she said it that she would regret the words. "You know my predicament, my lord. There are certain monetary considerations—"

In a low hard tone, he demanded the truth, "And these monetary considerations, do they take precedence over any feelings you may have toward me?"

"Feelings are fleeting." She lifted her hand to emphasize her point, but it fluttered impotently back down to her lap. "One cannot dine on feelings, nor button them up against a chill."

"Eloquently said."

It was carefully constructed a litany. One she had recited to herself over and over during the previous year, as she convinced herself that she must marry to save her family from poverty. Elizabeth bowed her head feeling unaccountably ashamed.

"One last question, then I will not trouble you any further with my troublesome declarations."

Declarations? She glanced up. Were they? If only he had declared his love, she might have . . . what? Abandoned her family? No. Better that he hadn't forced her to make that choice.

"This afternoon . . ." She didn't look up, but she could hear him saying it through clenched teeth, "when you came so readily into my arms and willingly kissed me . . ." His shadow fell over her, blocking out the moonlight. "Did you feel nothing?"

I felt as if my soul might melt into yours. He would jeer at her for such a foolish notion.

Valen stepped back, waiting, as shafts of moonlight landed in her lap. Elizabeth stared at her useless hands, catching the silver of the moon, but unable to hold it. "It was . . . you . . ." She glanced up, desperate for him to understand without being forced to say the words.

"Exactly." He held out his arm and led her back to the gallery.

The ladies had just finished playing. His aunt sat in a chair facing the musicians and clapped enthusiastically.

Valen deposited Elizabeth into the chair next to Lady Alameda. "You must excuse me." He bowed to them. "The day's activities have wearied me."

The trio began playing a selection from Handel, a lovely melancholy sonata that twined around Elizabeth's frayed emotions like a choking vine.

Lady Alameda turned to her and whispered, "Made a muddle of it, did you, my dear?"

Elizabeth found she could not answer for fear the giant lump in her throat might suffocate her. A tear trickled down her cheek, a hot stinging tear. She dashed it away. Lady Alameda clucked her tongue in a wordless scold. And the gentle music wound tighter and tighter around Elizabeth's lonely soul.

Chapter 20

The Phantasmagorical Embroidery of Time

Her scream woke him, ripping through the thick quiet of the night with pure terror. Valen bolted upright, his heart pounding like gunfire.

Another of her nightmares. Devil take Merót!

The second scream was cut short. He threw back the blankets. She would wake the entire household. He jumped up and pulled on his trousers. Perhaps Biggs was right, maybe he ought to wear something to bed. It might save him time in situations like these. But a nightdress? He pulled on a shirt as he stumbled out of his room and down the hall toward her chamber.

"Elizabeth?" He pushed open her door.

She sat up in bed, trembling, her eyes wide, hugging her pillow, shaking her head at him. The curtain hung open, the window thrown wide, allowing a soft breeze to ruffle through the room. Moonlight trickled in from behind racing clouds.

She looked so terrified of him, Valen wondered if she might still be half asleep. Her face was nearly as white as the bedcovers. "Izzie? Don't be afraid, sweeting. It's only me. You're having another of your dreams."

"No!" She held out her hand warding him off, shaking her head frantically, gulping for air.

"Don't be frightened." Valen went to her and sat on the edge of the bed. He cupped her cheek, smoothing back her damp dark hair. "You're safe, Izzie."

"N-o." The simple word fell from her lips in two syllables, broken by gasps of air and fear. Her gaze darted to the gloom in the corner of the room and her panic intensified. Valen realized, too late, his error. He spun around.

From the shadows, he emerged. "An' interesting tableau, eh?" A pistol leveled at them.

"Merót."

"The same." He inclined his head. "Good evening, Monsieur Hawk."

Valen reached back and pulled Izzie close behind him, keeping his body between her and the Frenchman. He kept his voice steady, fighting the fury swelling up inside him. "I see you evaded my men in London."

"Evaded? Ha! I strolled out of London without the least hint of trouble. You British, you are so arrogant. So deliciously overconfident." He kissed his fingers and threw it at them, chuckling. "Your king is insane. Your prince is a fat idiot. Your people are hungry. And still, you think you rule the world. Bah! Soon you will see—you are nothing but a pathetic little island."

Valen eased off the bed, keeping Elizabeth behind him. "You may have escaped for now, but my men will soon be on your scent."

"Ah. So, you think you are the hunter, no? *The infamous Red Hawk.* You would do well to remember the *renard*, the fox, *n'est pas?* He is a hunter as well." No more flippancy in his tone, his voice resonated with challenge. "And so we meet, the hawk and the fox, over this fearful little rabbit. Who shall have her for dinner, I wonder."

Valen took a step toward Merót, still shielding Elizabeth. "She has nothing to do with any of this."

"Oh no? You think not? She is all part of the game. All part of the hunt, yes? The lure."

"She wasn't a spy, if that's what you think. Purely an accident that our paths crossed at Smythe's."

"I do not believe in accidents." Merót shrugged. "Fate, perhaps. It does not matter. She is the bait, which brings us together. And now the fox will devour the hawk."

He took another step. "Very well, let us settle this between ourselves. I will meet you outside."

"How very convenient for you. But no. I wish to have bunny for dessert." He smiled and bobbed the pistol in Valen's direction. "Kindly stay where you are. I did not make the mistake of bringing a single shot this time. As you can see, I have two bullets—one for you, and one for our rabbit."

Valen frowned at the over and under. Would one shot from the small pistol drop him? He doubted it. But, if it did, Izzie would fall next. He had to think of something.

"I think you will find Lady Elizabeth is not the helpless little creature you perceive her to be. Why do you think she sleeps alone at her great age?"

Even in their situation, she would huff up. He

could envision the indignant pucker on her brow and it brought a twitch to the corner of his mouth.

He had piqued Merót's curiosity. Valen crossed his arms casually, to put the Frenchman off guard. "No. She's no rabbit. More of a marmot."

"Ha!" Merót waved his hand to Elizabeth. "You see, the insensitive Englishman—he insults you, my lady. This marmot, it is a ground squirrel, no?"

"Yes," she muttered plaintively. Valen felt her lean her forehead against his back.

He grinned. "A unique creature—the marmot. Deceptive. She has hidden fangs and claws." He demonstrated the claws coming out. "And her tongue . . ." Valen shook his head gravely. "It is pure poison."

"*C'est la vie,* it is thus with all women." Merót shrugged, unimpressed. "This is foolishness—"

"Ah. But, this marmot is deadly. A man doesn't stand a chance. At night, she climbs up into the trees, waiting for her unsuspecting quarry, and then—"

Elizabeth guessed what he planned to do. Rather than a marmot leaping, it would be Valen. Surely, Merót would see it coming. How could he not?

A shot blasted through the darkness. Roaring with death. And then another blast. And another. Blazing orange flashes. Elizabeth clamped her hands over her ears and screamed. Valen would fall on her. Dead.

Three shots. Three. It made no sense. Elizabeth dropped her hands. Her mind skipped around in time. What had happened? A flash of light from the door. She turned. Lord Ransley teetered in the entrance, a pistol in his hand, smoke curling around the double barrels.

He coughed, grabbing the top of a chair to balance himself, and fought back a spasm, faltering as he stumbled forward to stand over the fallen body of the Frenchman.

"Good evening, son. Does this finish up your *small administrative affair?*" he asked cynically and nudged the dead man with his toe. "One to the head. Thought I missed that first shot." He glanced up at his son. "You were too long-winded by half, Valen. Thought you were never going to make your play."

"If you'd waited . . ." Valen's arm went around Elizabeth, hugging her to his side. He murmured in her ear, "Are you unharmed?"

She nodded, and saw it then, a red stain, spreading on his white shirt. Her throat seized.

His face bent to hers, his mouth moved in soft sounds that twisted her stomach in answering pain.

"The marmot wins," he whispered and chuckled faintly before he collapsed.

"Dear God, no!" she cried out. "No. Valen!"

Elizabeth caught him as he collapsed against her.

Funny, Valen had thought, how everything slows to a crawl in moments like these. He'd seen it before, on the continent in the heat of battle.

He had spotted his father in the doorway, bracing himself for a shot. Time began to crawl. Valen heard the hammer fall, glimpsed the tiny spark, and saw the fire flare out from the barrel of the gun. The pistol sang out and the ball struck its mark.

What Valen didn't expect was the blaze that spouted from the end of Merót's gun as the Frenchman fell back. A bolt of light streaked in his direction. A second shot bellowed from his father's gun and brought the Fox down.

Izzie's screams resonated off the walls, stabbing his eardrums, making him want to shout to silence her. Just when he figured he would be deaf for a fortnight, a voice penetrated his numbness.

"Thought you would never make your play." It was his father, scolding him for waiting too long, his voice slow, protracted, his motions distant, removed, as if Valen watched it all from the end of a murky spyglass. His ears hummed, buzzed.

Fire burned in his upper chest. He glanced down and saw the ring of blood. He'd been hit. Instantly, he turned, fearing the ball might have passed through him and struck Izzie as well.

He put his arm around her. She seemed steady, but ghostly white in the milky illumination from the window.

He could no longer stand straight. The effort cost too much. So he leaned against her, hoping to smell her sweet scent instead of the acrid gunpowder. Allowing his head to droop toward her neck, he breathed in one more time. *Vanilla and roses.* He would take the memory of it with him to the place consigned for him in the next life.

"The marmot wins," he whispered, thinking it somehow funny. But, she didn't laugh. Her stricken expression whipped him. His strength whistled away.

The last thing Valen felt before blackness overtook him was the incredible softness of her breast against his cheek as he slid down toward a whirling abyss. She called to him, but he had no power to answer.

Some defiant part of him fought to hold on—tightening his grip on the thin cotton of her nightdress. If only he might stay, a moment longer, he would die and be satisfied. She cried out his name. It sounded so very far away. *Vanilla and roses. Raven black hair. The face of their son that did not yet exist. Her breast against his cheek.* All these images swirled together, spinning faster, and faster, until the whirling gray swallowed him up.

Chapter 21

Darning

Elizabeth managed to heave Valen onto her bed. The room filled with servants, lighting lamps, exclaiming over the shocking scene, and Lord Ransley fell into a coughing fit.

Elizabeth ripped open Valen's shirt. A bloody hole above his left breast marred his broad chest. She whimpered, unable to hold back the small cries that kept coming from her throat. Charred skin and the smell of blood curdled her nostrils. The familiar bilge in her stomach began to rise, but she shoved fear aside and gritted her teeth. *No! No time for that nonsense.* Anger that this should happen to him, and an overwhelming determination to set it right drove her forward.

Lady Alameda charged into the bedroom, her hair awry and an expression on her face that would have put Medusa to the blush. "Good God! What happened? Is he dead?"

Elizabeth didn't know if the countess referred to her nephew or the Frenchman on the floor, and she had neither the time nor the inclination to look at Merót. *No time to be sick.* "Send for a doctor," Elizabeth ordered.

"You heard her, man. Go! Send a rider to fetch the sawbones and hurry up about it." Lady Alameda shoved a manservant out of the door. She turned to her brother. "William, what are you doing out of bed?"

Lord Ransley's coughing subsided. He stooped over breathing heavily, a kerchief pressed to his lips. "Lad was in a bit of a tangle."

"So I see. Excellent shooting."

Lord Ransley had no interest in surveying his marksmanship. He shuffled toward Elizabeth. "How bad is it?"

Elizabeth cautiously slid her hand under Valen's shoulder, probing to see if the bullet had passed through. It hadn't. She sighed, bowing her head as she answered, "I pray it did not hit his lung. But the lead is still lodged in his shoulder."

For a moment, she thought grief would over-take the frail lord, but his countenance suddenly turned resolute. "Honore! Tell the rider . . . Tell him I will pay a hundred sovereigns if he carries the doctor back within the hour."

Lady Alameda wasted no time. She ran to the window and leaned out. "You there!" She relayed Lord Ransley's promise to the messenger as he ran to the stables. Indeed, the lady's voice bellowed with such force Elizabeth calculated half of Britain had heard the offer.

"What shall we do in the meantime?" Elizabeth pulled a blanket up over Valen thinking his quaking meant he must be cold.

Lady Alameda turned from the window. "We'll need some whiskey. And you there—build a fire. We'll want potash if the wound turns sour."

Lord Ransley dropped resignedly into a chair. "Cart that vermin out of here." He waved at Merót's body.

Servants sprang forward to rid the room of the Fox's remains.

"I should have acted more quickly." Lord Ransley lowered his head into his hands.

"Don't!" His sister commanded and patted his shoulder. "He will not die. Far too stubborn, our Valen. You have my word on it."

He glanced up at the wild-haired countess. Hope flickering in his eyes with the temerity of a candle standing in a breeze. "Would that I could hold you to it."

Valen groaned.

"Laudanum. Find some laudanum." Lady Alameda clapped her hands at the maid who was on her knees wiping up blood from the floor. "Run girl."

Elizabeth held Valen down while Lady Alameda poured hot whiskey into the wound. He roared like a lion. His eyes flew open, but they were wild and unseeing. Both women nearly landed on the floor when he fought them off.

After she regained her equilibrium, Lady Alameda adjusted her bed jacket and leaned cautiously over their delirious patient. She glanced up at Elizabeth. "Clearly, I didn't dose him enough."

It seemed impossible considering the amount they'd forced him to swallow.

At that moment, the doctor arrived, his clothing

askew, his hair mussed, looking as if he'd been snatched out of bed, thrust on a horse, and hauled across the countryside with the devil nipping his heels. Which must have been exactly what happened.

He blinked when he entered the brightly lit room, gripping a leather case in one hand and an apothecary box in the other. "What happened?"

Lady Alameda exhaled loudly. "For pity's sake! Don't stand there gawking. He's been shot. The ball is still in and you must take it out." It sounded like such a simple thing, like removing a loaf of baked bread from the oven.

It would not be simple. Elizabeth dreaded the procedure, but it must be done. She vowed she would not get sick. She would see it through. Assist in whatever way she might.

The gentleman didn't look much of a doctor, a pock-faced middle-aged man, far too reluctant as he peeked at his patient. "Fellow this size—we'll need a couple strong lads to hold him down."

Lady Alameda had her hands on her hips. "I dosed him quite heavily with laudanum."

"So I see." He pulled up Valen's eyelids and checked the pupils. "Ought to have waited until after. But never mind. We'll still need two men."

Lord Ransley coughed and added in a hoarse voice, "I'll triple your customary fee if he lives."

The hesitant doctor was not immune to this incentive. "Right." Suddenly more confident, he rolled up his sleeves and frowned at his benefactor. "Lord Ransley, you ought to return to bed. It'll do no good to stay here. The strain will be too much for you. I cannot cope with two crises at once." He opened the latch on his leather case and displayed a frightening set of instruments. "As soon as the procedure is complete, I shall bring you a full accounting."

Lord Ransley struggled to rise. "So be it, but I insist you report to me as soon as possible." Lady Alameda assisted her brother back to his room.

The surgeon turned to Elizabeth. "And you, young lady, off to bed as well. This is no place for the faint of heart."

"This *is* my bed." Elizabeth straightened her shoulders and elevated her chin stubbornly. "And I am certainly not fainthearted," she lied. "I'm staying."

A few minutes later, she wondered if she hadn't been a trifle hasty. The doctor selected several gruesome-looking tools and placed them on the bed table. He raised a long slender probe and directed two footmen to hold Lord St. Cleve up in a sitting position. Then, he began the grisly search for the bullet and any other matter that might have been carried into the wound.

Valen groaned in agony, clenching his teeth. The footmen tightened their grip, although, amazingly, he seemed to be cooperating.

"Surely, he can't be conscious?" Elizabeth held her hand over her heart and pressed down, in a feeble attempt to control the rapid beating.

"In and out, I expect." The doctor plucked out a small bloody corner of fabric and shook it onto the floor. "A soldier, wasn't he? They know what to expect. Look at this! Struck the bone, but didn't break it all the way." His elbow cocked up as he elevated his angle, digging deeper in Valen's chest.

Valen bellowed like an angry bull. Elizabeth expected at any minute that the two footmen and the doctor would be sent flying across the room. But Valen only rolled his head back, his eyes squeezed tightly shut, growling.

"Right! Got it." The surgeon pulled out a splinter of bone and smiled as if he'd discovered a gold nugget among the muscle and gore, before returning to his work.

Bile rose in Elizabeth's throat. She held her stomach and turned away.

"Hand me that one." Without looking at her, the doctor waved his fingers at his array of instruments. "Quickly. The long extractor."

She took a deep breath, ignored her stupid stomach, and gave him the long thin pincers, bracing herself for Valen's next cry of pain. But his head bowed forward, sweat drenched strands of gold and fire falling beside his agonized features. She clamped her trembling lips together and sent desperate prayers to heaven.

The doctor muttered to himself and fished deeper for the ball. At last, he withdrew, holding a misshapen bullet in his forceps. He inspected it before plunking it down on the table. "Looks to be in one piece."

Blood cascaded in a steady stream down Valen's chest. "Thread that needle with the silk." He pointed at a card wrapped with white thread. "And call for more rags."

He pulled a small cylindrical flask from his apothecary, poured some of the yellow powder onto a slip of paper, curved the parchment, and funneled the contents into Valen's wound. "Piece of good luck it didn't hit the lung. A near thing."

Elizabeth's hand shook as she aimed a length of silk suture at the eye of a wickedly curved needle. She couldn't help but envision the point stabbing into Valen's flesh. Piercing the very shoulder she had rested her head against and felt so comforted and safe.

If only I hadn't screamed.

She would be dead and he might be spared. It had all happened so quickly, before she had time to think. She awoke and Merót stood beside her bed leering at her. The scream tore out of her throat, unbidden.

Who could have known Valen would be the one to hear? The one to race to her bedchamber? Merót must have guessed—vile fox. She bit down hard on the corner of her lip to suppress her tears. *If only I hadn't screamed.*

She handed the doctor the threaded needle.

Five loose stitches, the doctor did not close the wound completely. "Seepage," he explained, and unscrewed a jar of leeches. Three, he placed on top of the oozing wound.

Elizabeth cringed at the dark sluglike creatures.

"Stops the bleeding," the doctor claimed.

She grimaced, skeptical that anything so repulsive might serve a beneficial purpose.

"I have it on good authority, Napoleon's surgeons use them on the battlefield all the time."

A recommendation she could do without. She wished never to hear of another Frenchman as long as she lived.

After the servants mopped up the blood, and they padded the bed with extra linen and laid Valen back against a mound of pillows, Elizabeth whispered to the surgeon, "Will he live?" A foolish question. Who but God, could answer?

"It's possible. The extraction went well." He rubbed at his scraggily side-whiskers and stared at their patient. "I must report to Lord Ransley."

She nodded and sat down to have a good cry.

Chapter 22

The Torn Tapestry of Foolish Dreams

Silent tears choked her, assailed her complexion, running in salty streams, crumpling her already haggard face. Wrinkles and lines no longer mattered to her. *I should not have screamed.* If she hadn't, Elizabeth might be in the next world with her father. Where he would have the pleasure of scolding her for eternity and telling her exactly how she ought to have behaved. Instead, the useless marmot lived on—a mean waddling ground squirrel with claws and a poison tongue.

She stood up and brushed away the tears as she went to him. Her fingers gently trailed over the muscles of his arm. Why would he die to protect a wretched little marmot?

Elizabeth heard a commotion downstairs and didn't care. The world might come crashing down around her ears. It didn't matter. If Valen didn't survive, none of it mattered. She wondered how she could ever have been so foolish to think she might trade her heart to repair the family fortune. She would be no different from her father—chasing after money and neglecting those who really mattered.

Clattering outside the door, men talking, the sound of boots reporting on the stone stairs—none of it interested her.

She lightly brushed back Valen's wavy hair.

"Izzie!"

"Robert?" She turned.

In three strides, her brother was at her side. "I failed you. The blighter got away from me."

None of that mattered. "It's over." All that mattered was the future.

Robert still blustered his excuses. "Lost Merót's trail on the outskirts of London. Had a feeling he'd come here. But we had to check all of the possibilities. It took too long. Then, I heard that wretched screaming in my head and I knew." He patted her. "Izzie! Izzie! Stop crying."

She hadn't realized she was. Robert clasped her shoulders and gave her a shake. She suddenly became aware there were two soldiers in the room with them and fought to compose herself.

Robert let go of her and turned to Valen. "How is he?"

"He has a chance." She pressed her lips together to stop the trembling, before attempting to say more. "The bullet didn't strike his lung."

Robert studied Valen as if he might divine the future if he stared hard enough. "That's all right then, isn't it? If there's any chance at all, the Captain here will take full advantage."

His men murmured in agreement.

"Yes. He'll pull through." Robert brought himself to attention, blind bravado filling his chest. "Not the sort to give up, is he."

"Not bloody likely. Begging yer pardon, mum. Like as not the Captain would give ole St. Peter a taste of his fives and march straight back down to earth."

She turned at the familiar voice and was startled to see Lord St. Cleve's unlikely servant, looking much more likely in a soldier's uniform. He tipped his shako and bowed. "Don't you worry, miss. His Grace has enough backbone for three men."

The others agreed.

His Grace. Some muddled part of her mind felt compelled to correct him. *He's not a duke.* But she silenced the babbling marmot. Valen was far more noble than any duke she knew. Let the man call him his grace.

Robert nudged her. "See here, Izzie. Watch over St. Cleve, will you? I've got to take this lot and haul Merót's carcass back to Whitehall. There are several gentlemen there, very anxious to see the rascal has been recovered."

"Must you leave so soon?"

He nodded, kissed her cheek, and he and his men stormed out as suddenly as they had entered.

The room lay silent, but not nearly as bleak as it had been before her brother arrived.

Lady Alameda glided in and stood beside Elizabeth at Valen's bedside. "His color is passable." She prodded her nephew with one finger. He stirred in response and then sank back into his stupor. "Out till tomorrow I expect. And I, for one, have had enough excitement for one evening. It's back to bed for me. Surely you don't intend to stand here all night staring at him."

"I doubt I could sleep."

"Perhaps not, but you ought to try. You look positively ghastly my dear, like you've been dragged through a briar patch."

An interesting compliment coming from a lady whose uncombed hair resembled a thistle gone to seed. "Thank you. I shall take it under advisement."

"Yes. Well, good! Go ahead and lay down then."

"A small problem."

The countess arched a brow and waited.

"There is a rather large man in my bed."

"It is a very big bed."

Elizabeth drew back, a hand to her breast. "Are you suggesting?"

"I'm suggesting you get some rest." Lady Alameda sniffed imperiously. "I daresay we've taxed the servants enough for one night. Rather than selfishly rouse an army of them to attend to your needs, simply because you are too—"

"Surely, not in the same bed?"

"Pooh. Don't be so miss-ish. He's unconscious. What could happen?"

"No." All the lessons from her youth screamed at her. Her father's birch rod waved an invisible warning in front of her face. "It wouldn't be at all proper."

"Good heavens, child. If you're concerned about the proprieties, you may come sleep with me in my room. But I warn you—I have no wish to be woken up again until the sun is well up tomorrow." Lady Alameda crossed her arms and thrummed the toe of her slipper on the floor. "I daresay, you will insist on pattering down here every ten minutes to see how he fares."

She was right. Elizabeth wouldn't be able to sleep for worrying about whether he was catching fever, or in pain. "Very well. I'll sleep in the chair."

"My dear, there is only one chair and the doctor plans to use that one as soon as he has put my brother at ease." Lady Alameda glanced sharply around the room and pointed. "Well, I suppose you might use that little writing chair at the desk. Really, Elizabeth, be practical. The doctor makes a perfectly proper chaperone."

Elizabeth went and got the straight back wooden chair and plunked it firmly on the floor beside the bed.

"Suit yourself." Honore shrugged and bent to kiss her nephew on the forehead. "Stubborn boy." She ruffled back his newly shorn hair and murmured, "If you weren't my favorite nephew I might be quite peeved at you for putting us through all this turmoil."

Valen remained silent.

Lady Alameda straightened and cast a viperous look at Elizabeth. "It is well you plan to watch over him. Should anything happen to him, I might be tempted to blame you for all this." Then her features cooled as rapidly as they had turned vicious. She smiled coyly at Elizabeth. "Pleasant dreams."

Lady Alameda meandered slowly out of the room, turning out the extra lanterns as she went, blowing out candles. She stopped in the doorway and turned. "He really is a fine specimen, is he not?"

"Good night, my lady."

The countess laughed and the wicked sound of it echoed down the hall as she walked away. Elizabeth shook her head.

* * *

A few minutes later, the doctor assisted Lord Ransley into the room. "You see. It is precisely as I told you. Lord St. Cleve is resting comfortably." The physician checked Valen's pulse.

Lord Ransley stared at his son, hesitantly brushing the side of Valen's face with his knuckles. A sliver of water ran down the father's gaunt cheek and sluiced down into the lace of his collar. "You must get well," he whispered. Then he turned his head away to cough.

"You've expended your energies, my lord." The doctor placed his hands on Lord Ransley's shoulders and tried to guide him away. "You can do no more for him tonight."

Valen's father was not ready to be ushered away. Elizabeth touched his sleeve. "Thank you, my lord, for saving us. We would be dead, if it were not for you."

Lord Ransley pressed his hand over hers and met her gaze. "Do all you can for him. I've seen the way he looks at you. If he knows you are here . . . perhaps . . ." Under the weight of his despair the gray rings under Lord Ransley's eyes burrowed deeper with each passing minute. "Please. He is all I have that matters."

She nodded, an answering tightness in her chest making it impossible to speak.

"Come, my lord. You must rest." The doctor prevailed upon him and, patting the frail man's shoulders, took Lord Ransley away. He returned with a fresh bowl of water and a stack of white linen rags. "His Lordship tells me you are a healer—familiar with herbs."

"Only in passing, sir."

He nodded. "Just as well, one must remember,

some of those old remedies do more harm than good."

She nodded obediently, but wondered, somewhat annoyed, how a man who just set three hideous leeches to suck on Valen's chest might judge the validity of using a little garlic to strengthen the lungs.

"However, I'm glad you know something about tending the infirm." He set down his supplies and scratched at his side-whiskers. "We must ward off fever. Throughout the night, it is essential to wet these cloths and wipe him down every hour or so." He opened his watch and set it on the table beside the pan of water. "I shall be glad of your assistance."

He showed her how to do it and then sat down in the padded armchair. Stretching out his legs, he crossed them at the ankles, yawned, stretched, propped his head to one side and promptly dozed off. Obviously, he was quite used to sleeping in a chair.

Elizabeth had no such similar success. The writing chair was hard and the wooden back annoyed her spine when she tried to lean back. She got up and rummaged through her belongings until she found a book. She pulled it out, squinted at the title, and wished she might find something more stimulating than a book of lectures on the proper conduct of young ladies. She dug again and produced a book of Shakespearean sonnets.

As much as she admired William Shakespeare, his poetry did not prove as riveting as she had hoped. Her head drooped and the text blurred. At last, she stopped struggling and closed the small volume.

She turned down the remaining lamp, leaving

just enough dusky light to radiate over their patient. She sat down and stared at Valen. Soon the silence teemed with small sounds, his erratic breathing, the tick, tick, ticking of the pocket watch as it resonated against the table. The steady undulation of the doctor's snores as they fluttered and whistled, going in and out against his heavy mustache.

Elizabeth massaged the ache in her neck and shoulders, and leaned back, hoping to close her eyes and ease some of her weariness.

Valen murmured, a loud garbled set of consonants Elizabeth couldn't comprehend. She checked the time and it surprised her that an hour had passed so quickly.

Checking his brow for fever, she sighed with relief to find he was not too hot. She drenched a rag and wrung it out to wipe him down. The task passed quickly. Once more she returned to the small chair and resumed her vigil.

Some time later, she awoke, her chin bowed against her chest, surprised to find she had drowsed. Valen thrashed his head from side to side, muttering incoherently. She tapped on the clock to make sure it was working correctly, finding it hard to believe she had slept so long. She prepared another wet cloth.

When she pulled down the bedsheet, Valen grabbed her wrist and his eyes flashed open, glazed, wild. Elizabeth knew at once that he was not seeing her, but some phantom.

"Leave her be, Merót!" He tried to shout, but it came out in the husky half whisper of a nightmare.

"Shhh." Elizabeth crooned, wiping his brow. "It's over. Merót is dead. It's over."

He let go of her and rocked his head from side

to side. "Izzie," he muttered, and drifted back into a fitful sleep.

She bathed the sweat from his neck and carefully dabbed away the crusting blood at the outer edges of his wound, flinching at the sight of the pulsating brown-black leeches. She averted her eyes from the grotesque creatures and softly ran the rag over the muscles of his abdomen.

An irony, that so much power should lay helpless, dormant beneath her fingers. She traced her fingertips lightly over the powerful ridges. When they contracted under her touch, a jolt of heat flamed into her cheeks. *A lady ought not touch such a man thus. Especially an unconscious man. No! Any man. Conscious or not.* Elizabeth glanced guiltily at the doctor. *Undoubtedly, you ought to have selected the* Lectures on Proper Conduct for Young Ladies *to read.*

Her chaperone snored rhythmically, completely at peace. The house might burn down and she guessed he would sleep through it. Oh, yes, he was a perfectly proper chaperone.

Elizabeth quickly pulled Valen's covers up, and straightened her aching shoulders. She was exhausted. Otherwise, she never would have ventured to ... to what? All she did was merely wipe down a feverish patient. Yes. She was making *much ado about nothing.* Precisely. She would adhere to Mr. Shakespeare's wisdom and not make molehills out of nothing. Or something along those lines. Gad. She was tired.

Elizabeth plopped down on the hard chair. The pocket watch ticked. The doctor's mustache quivered as he snored. The oil lamp hissed and flickered because she'd set it so low. Valen muttered in his sleep. And she stared down at her toes and wondered how she would get through the night. She decided to make a game for herself, and squinted at the tapestry hanging on the wall behind the doctor. It was a medieval hunting scene. How many antelope did the lords and ladies chase? How many whippets with lovely arched necks surrounded the hunters? How many horses . . .

Perhaps, she might just rest her head on the edge of his bed, use it as a pillow of sorts, to add a bit of comfort while she sat. Elizabeth curled her arm up beside her head and fell asleep.

"Izzie?" Valen asked, his voice groggy. "What are you doing in hell?"

Her eyes blinked open. She struggled to comprehend, and sat up, rubbing her eyes. "We're not in hell, dearest. You're alive."

He dragged down the sheet and stared at his wound.

She jumped up and tried to cover him up, but he stopped her.

"Not in hell? Then, what are these demons doing on me?" He snatched off two of the leeches and threw them across the room. The engorged slugs splattered against the tapestry and oozed down the stone wall.

"No. Valen you shouldn't. The doctor said they will stop the bleeding."

He yanked the third leech off. The sucking sound made her flinch.

"Saw injured men who ought to have lived, sucked to death by these vermin." He hurled the wiggling creature.

Elizabeth watched in horror as it plopped onto the doctor's shirt, who stirred and brushed at his mustache as if a mosquito had flown past.

"No," she whispered. "The doctor should decide. I'll wake him."

Valen grabbed her arm. "Don't bother. I won't allow it anyway."

The stunned leech came to life and slithered across the physician's waistcoat leaving a trail of red

Elizabeth shook her head. "I ought to wake him." At the very least, she ought to retrieve that leech before it found a new home on the physician. But, that would mean picking it up. She wrinkled her nose. With a tiny bit of good fortune, the hideous thing would simply crawl away and die.

Valen tugged on her arm. "No cutting. No leeches. Promise me."

She leaned over him, he seemed so very tired, but it was a marvel to see the familiar stubbornness back in his eyes. She attempted to protest. "But surely the doctor knows—"

"Promise." He tugged her closer.

She had no power to deny him—he might ask anything and she would do it. "Very well. I promise."

The shadow of a smile curved his lips and Valen closed his eyes. "That's my little marmot."

"On second thought—" she bristled, but he had fallen back into oblivion again.

Elizabeth wiped him down with a fresh cloth, covered him up, and settled back in the chair. This time, making no pretense of trying to stay awake, she rested both arms on the edge of his mattress, laid her head down, and closed her eyes.

"Izzie?" Valen whispered.

She glanced up. His hand groped out from under the bedding, reaching for her. She slipped her hand under his palm. Valen took a deep breath and closed his fingers around hers. They both drifted contentedly back to sleep.

Chapter 23

To Hem or Not to Hem

Morning whiskered its way under her eyelids, but Elizabeth brushed it away. She was too tired to care what time it was. Valen's hand was still warm as he held hers. Like pesky mayflies, voices buzzed softly in the room, disturbing the edge of Elizabeth's slumber. In her drowsy state, she wondered if angels had come to watch over Valen as he slept.

"An interesting couple, are they not?"

"Yes."

"Ill suited from the very beginning."

"How so?"

"Too much alike, I'd say."

He sighed deeply. "And yet . . ."

"And yet, quite opposite in many respects."

"Hmm." He coughed.

"Precisely," she declared triumphantly. "Just enough trouble to keep life interesting. Perfect. A match made in heaven."

"I'd prefer if they stay on earth for the time being. I want a grandson."

"Don't worry." She chuckled wickedly. "I daresay, they'll be littering the manor house with a brood of hellions in no time."

Elizabeth's mind fluttered, she recognized that mischievous cackle and it certainly didn't belong to any angel. She raised her head and struggled to get her bearings.

Lord Ransley laughed and it turned into a cough.

"Good morning, my dear," Lady Alameda cooed. "I see you observed the proprieties. Perched in that pathetic little chair the entire night. And you probably have a stiff neck to show for it."

She was right, of course. Elizabeth rubbed at the neck in question, while the doctor still snored and probably hadn't budged all night. She wondered where the evil little leech had gotten off to. In a fleeting panic, she checked her ankles. To her great relief, she did not find an ugly globular worm sucking on either of her legs.

Springing up, she checked Valen's color and folded down the sheets to make certain the wound was not festering.

Lady Alameda put her hands on Elizabeth's shoulders and pulled her back. "Why don't you go and wash up dear. I had the servants move your things to a room down the hall."

Had she slept through all of that? Still. She couldn't leave him. "No. I . . ."

"Elizabeth. There are others to care for him now. You must tend to your own needs for the moment."

She shook her head. "No. I have to stay. I gave him my word. No bloodletting. No more leeches. He made me swear to it."

"Yes. I see he dashed the little darlings against the wall." She glanced pointedly at the tapestry. "You mustn't worry. I will see to it that your promise is kept. Isn't that correct, doctor?" She kicked out with her right shoe and connected with the physician's foot.

"What? What?" he sputtered. "Certainly." The surgeon stood up, adjusting his waistcoat and jacket. "Wretched mosquitoes." He grimaced and swatted at his calf before snatching his watch from the bed table, and tapping on it. "Is that the time?" He wound it and clipped it back onto his waistcoat, itching at his pant leg with the toe of his shoe.

Elizabeth hadn't noticed any mosquitoes and suspected the doctor would soon discover the whereabouts of his missing leech. She left Lady Alameda to deal with his ire.

Valen stirred to the faint sound of his father's laughter, a sound that seemed more a dream than reality.

Through half-opened eyelids, he glanced to his side and found the place where Izzie had laid her head during the night. *Empty.* Valen sighed and closed his eyes. He had hoped to see her face, see again the concern in her blue eyes. Witness the affection in her gaze. She loved him—it was undeniable. He vowed she would fill that empty place in his bed as soon as possible.

He had to convince her. If necessary, he would trick her into it. As a last resort, he'd abduct her and carry his stubborn bride off to Gretna Green. Considering the condition of his shoulder, he hoped one of the less strenuous methods would serve.

The alternative was unthinkable. No Izzie in his

bed. And if she should foolishly accept some wealthy nodcock, well then he would have to commit murder. All the hounds of hell could not prevail upon him to allow that milksop, Horton, to have her. Nor would he give her up to anyone else.

He drowsed, unwilling to surrender completely to sleep. He had no wish to return to unpredictable dreams in Morpheus's jurisdiction. His father's quiet murmur nudged him toward greater waking.

"Yes, it's true. His grandfather robbed the secondary title. Aha! Black bishop takes your knight."

"A pity. Why, Lord Ransley, how very generous. You left my rook open to take your bishop."

Valen's eyelids fluttered. She was here. He blinked, squinting against the brightness. They sat by the window, his father and Izzie, a chessboard spread on the table between them.

"Neatly done, my lady." His father coughed. "Hmm. I will consider my next move more carefully."

Valen watched sunbeams twirling in a shaft of warm yellow light from the window. *Extraordinary.* Perhaps, he was still dreaming.

"Queen's pawn, one step." His father's voice sounded real enough. "Did he not tell you about his allowance?"

"No. We've never spoken of such private matters. Naturally, I assumed it was modest given your father's divestiture."

"Oh no. I saw to it he receives a handsome settlement. I wished to correct my father's—"

"Best not give the marmot such juicy tidbits," Valen interrupted before his father divulged all. He wanted her, but he would have her on his own terms, not because of her mercenary streak.

"Oh dear." Lord Ransley clucked his tongue. "He's delirious again."

"Not this time." Izzie stood up and came to him smiling. "I believe you will find your son has finally returned to his right mind. He is simply indulging in his favorite pastime. Insulting me."

Valen laughed, an activity that hurt like hell.

"Welcome back to the land of the living, my lord." She took his hand and he grinned at her.

"Good morning, Marmot."

"I suggest, if you wish to remain alive, you will cease to use that name when referring to me."

"It is good to see you've not lost your bite."

"And you. How do you feel?"

A well meant, but absurd question. Unfortunately, her inquiry caused him to examine the facts. "As if Satan himself has run me through with a blazing spear. And you may tell my aunt, as kindly as you like, that I will have her put in chains and thrust into a dungeon if she ever dares administer laudanum to me again."

"Oh my." Izzie reared back, but he could see she was feigning her protest. "I didn't realize the manor had a dungeon, my lord."

His father stood at the end of the bed, leaning against one of the posts, looking to be in surprising good health. "Daresay, if we had a dungeon, my dear sister would have been locked away decades ago."

Valen mused that not many weeks had passed since he had been standing at his father's bed.

"As it is, Honore runs free, wreaking what havoc she may on everyone around her." His father shrugged happily. "You may be certain, my boy, she intends no harm."

"Not certain at all. Trapped me in a bloody nightmare. Thought I might never escape."

"She is rather free with the stuff." Izzie wrung out a cloth and washed his forehead. "I feared she might kill you, she gave you so much the first night."

"First night?" He frowned. "Wasn't that last night? The night you . . ."

The expressions on their faces gave Valen his answer. Obviously, his meddlesome aunt had dosed him with more opiates since. "How long has she kept me in this stupor?"

"Three days," she whispered and wiped his temples.

"And Merót?"

"Dead. Do you not remember?"

He leaned up on his good shoulder. "Paper and ink. I must send word to Robert. The authorities need a report."

"Robert was already here." Her voice flowed over him, as soothing as the warm cloth she glided along the side of his neck. "You needn't trouble yourself. He and his men took Merót's body away." She gently pressed him back to the pillows. "Lady Alameda gave them a full accounting of the events."

He groaned and tried to sit up again. "In that case, it is even more urgent I send word. You know how she is."

"You must eat first." Elizabeth smiled at him, a smile that drenched him in satisfaction.

Satisfaction notwithstanding, he had his duty to perform. "You don't understand."

"I understand perfectly."

He sighed. "If you did, you would comprehend the imperative nature of—"

"I will strike you a bargain. If you eat first, I will act as your scribe, and you may send word to whomever you wish in all haste."

His stomach rumbled, and he considered her offer. She was wearing the green muslin, the same one she'd worn that day at the ruins. He could remember the feel of her in his arms. If he played his hand artfully, he might gain more out of this bargain than a meal and a dispatch.

"I'm afraid it's out of the question," he said softly as she leaned close, bathing his shoulder. "I'm too unsteady yet to feed myself. If you will be kind enough to bring me something to drink, that will suffice."

She handed him a glass of water from the bed table, and frowned at him skeptically. "And yet, you contemplated writing?"

Clever marmot. He pinched his brow together, struggling to compose his features and disguise his ulterior motive. "I hadn't considered the matter thoroughly."

"Very well then. I will feed you."

He smiled.

If Valen had thought having Izzie dribble soup down his gullet would be romantic, he had erred. After the second time she dabbed at his mouth as if he were a helpless infant, he'd had enough. "Have you nothing of more substance? Meat for example? Something I might stab with one hand and eat on my own?"

His father, resting in the armchair, waved away his request. "The doctor said to introduce solids gradually."

"Hmm," he grumbled. "Doubt the Sawbones has ever gone three days without a proper meal."

Izzie perked up, an impish glint in her eyes. "This soup has meat. Only look for yourself, here is a knuckle bone." She held up a mangy boiled joint for his inspection.

"Not what I had in mind."

She set down the soup dish and stood up, brushing out her skirt. "Perhaps, my lord, if we were to bring you a leg of mutton you might hold it in your good hand and gnaw it to your heart's content?"

"That is ludicrous, surely he can't . . ." Lord Ransley frowned. "Oh, I see you're gibing him."

Yes. It was a ludicrous suggestion, even so, it sounded infinitely better than the butter and broth soup Elizabeth was feeding him.

"Exactly the thing," Valen ordered, with the same firmness he would command one of his soldiers. "That, and a firkin of wine, will serve admirably."

"As you wish." She turned abruptly to leave.

He wondered if he had carried his surliness too far. "Wait. Izzie." He leaned over to reach for her, but the sudden movement sent a hot stabbing pain searing into his injured shoulder. He fell back holding his breath.

She rushed back to his side. "What happened?"

"Hunger pains." He tried to smile.

"I will get you something else," she said in earnest.

He groped for her hand and found it. "First, my sweeting, the letter? Please. Then I promise to swallow whatever you choose. Saving, of course, no more of that knuckle soup."

She arched her brow, but submissively went to the desk and sat down, selected a piece of parchment and dipped a quill into the ink. Valen dictated the details of that night to the best of his recollection, including the fact that he had noticed some movement in the shrubbery on that night, but had dismissed it as an animal.

"Do you really think it might have been him?" Izzie glanced up sharply. "I saw it, too, when we were . . ." She glanced uncomfortably in the direction of his father.

"Yes." Valen traced an invisible circle on the mattress with his finger. "When you were rejecting my offer."

"What's this?" his father sputtered, suddenly attentive. "You offered for her?"

"He did not." Izzie's chin and nose rose in their customary salute to the ceiling, which meant she was on the defensive.

Valen nodded. "She spurned me."

"It was not an offer," she insisted.

He arched one brow. "I asked you to marry me, did I not?"

"Yes, but . . ."

"He did?" Lord Ransley sat on the edge of his seat. "And you said no?"

"Not precisely." Izzie bowed her head into her hand, and grimaced.

"She did."

"May we, please, return to the letter?" She sniffed loudly.

Lord Ransley shook his head, and sat back, his brow furrowed as he contemplated first one and then the other. "You said no," he muttered.

"Rejected me out of hand."

"The letter?" She poised the quill.

"As you wish." Valen dictated the rest of his missive. "And in conclusion, Robert, if you will return to Ransley Keep at your earliest convenience, there is a matter of great urgency I must discuss with you."

She glanced up, inquisitive. He loved that bright falconlike look she acquired when she got wind of something. He loved, equally well, watching her suppress her keenness. "And what matter might that be?" she asked, careful not to affect too much interest.

"A private matter, my dear."

His father chuckled and fell into a coughing fit.

Three days went by, and Valen said nothing more to Elizabeth about her rejection of his suit. Whenever she broached the subject, he changed it. *Deuced hard.* But Valen thought he knew best how to handle his wily little marmot.

Hardest, were the interminable nights, when he lay awake from the pain, wishing desperately that she were next to him. Instead, he had the privilege of listening to one of the footmen, sitting vigil in the armchair, snuffle and snort uncomfortably throughout the long nights.

Pater and Thomas came to visit him on Monday, carrying a bushel of remedies that Meg insisted Lady Elizabeth administer to him. They both grinned at him as if they knew some secret he didn't.

"Well?" Pater finally asked. "Did you figure it out?"

Thomas chuckled quietly and shook his head. "Women."

"You told Thomas?"

"I didn't say anything he and Meg couldn't see for themselves."

"Writ all over you, lad."

Valen cocked a brow, signaling the end of their overly bold interrogation. "I may have come to a conclusion or two."

They exchanged knowing glances and the conversation turned to sheep and grain.

Tuesday morning, the doctor appeared and said he had rarely seen a wound heal up with such vigor and that it was finally ready for a proper dressing.

That evening, while Izzie was downstairs, Valen's father slipped into the room and sent the servant away. He sat on the edge of Valen's bed. "Well?" He crossed his arms. "How do you plan to do it?"

"My lord?"

"Capture your bride?"

"Capture . . . ? Sounds like a new game of some sort. You'll have to explain."

Lord Ransley coughed and frowned at Valen over his kerchief. "You know perfectly well what I mean."

The corner of Valen's mouth curled with pleasure. "Very well, my lord, since you have broached the subject. Perhaps I might prevail upon you to assist me in the matter? You see"—he glanced down at his bandaged shoulder—"there are one or two elements of my plan I am not disposed to take care of at the moment."

His father grinned. "Delighted, my boy."

For the first time in their lives, they bent their heads together for a common purpose. He and Valen conspired how they might bring Lady Elizabeth up to the mark.

"God help me, we wouldn't have to go through all this nonsense if she weren't the most obstinate female in all of Christendom."

"Ah well, she would need to be a trifle headstrong, wouldn't she, to manage you?"

"There is that." Valen shook his head. "Excessively managing, our Izzie. In point of fact, she would probably put Napoleon to shame if she had been born a man."

They laughed, plotted, and disagreed on some of the finer points of their strategy, but they were united in the effort—two warriors hunting a prize. At the end of an hour, Lord Ransley stood up and clapped a hand on Valen's good shoulder in a wordless commendation. The approval and pride in his expression spoke eloquently enough.

An unfamiliar tightness gathered in Valen's throat, he tried to clear it away, but it wouldn't go. He faltered in an effort to say something, and landed on an inane comment about his health. "You are looking well, *father*."

His father's chest swelled and Valen caught the glimmer of water in Ransley's eyes. "For the first time in decades, I am truly happy."

Valen understood. *All those years without my mother, his bride. And then, scorned by his foolish son.*

As Lord Ransley walked away, Valen clamped his jaw tight, restraining the unmanly emotions that threatened to undo him. *How could I have been so blind?*

Chapter 24

Cutting to the Heart of the Matter

Love rules the court, the camp, the grove, And men below, and saints above; For love is heaven, and heaven is love.—Sir Walter Scott, *The Lay of the Last Minstrel*, 1805

At long last, Robert arrived. Valen thought he would go mad waiting. He sat up in bed while Elizabeth read to him, a melancholy canto written by a fellow named Scott. It sounded like a tale about a dying soldier, but there were plenty of references to love in the verses. At these junctures, she was wont to pause and sigh pointedly, until it was all he could do to keep from grabbing the blasted book and heaving it across the room. So, when Robert strode in, Valen felt as if the sun had come out, even though the skies outside his window still boded rain.

"What the devil took you so long?" After endless days of confinement, this was the cheeriest greeting Valen could muster.

"Delighted to see you in such fine spirits, Valen." Robert clasped Valen's hand, gave it a jarring shake and then turned to greet his sister. "Has he been a great nuisance?"

"Exceedingly great." She marked the book and shut it. "I will leave you gentlemen. You must have many private matters you wish to discuss." She was not usually so eager to escape him.

"Wait, Elizabeth. This concerns you as well."

"But, I thought . . . ?"

His father entered carrying a long slender wooden case, set it on the desk, and opened it. A pair of foils nested in red velvet.

Robert hefted one of the blades, checking the weight and balance. "Excellent." He swished it out to his side, nearly connecting with the bedpost. "Superb balance. Where did you get them?"

"Italian. You may, of course, select your weapon."

Izzie whipped to attention like a beagle catching a scent. "What? What are you saying?"

Valen attempted to shrug, disregarding his bandaged shoulder. "Merely that your brother must challenge me."

Robert stopped testing the rapier. "Must I?"

"Afraid so. No choice in the matter."

Elizabeth's voice went up an octave. "On what grounds?"

He looked squarely at Robert. "I compromised her."

Izzie's mouth fell open and then snapped shut. "You did not." She turned to her brother and clutched his arm. "It isn't true, Robert. He didn't."

Robert patted her hand patiently. "I would think

he would know, my dear." He glanced over her head at Valen for confirmation. "Did you?"

"I did, on several occasions, take advantage and kiss her warmly." He stated the facts as if they were in court.

Robert's eyebrows rose. "Warmly?"

Valen nodded. "Warmly. Naturally, I offered for her."

"Right." Robert's posture relaxed. "Well, then the matter is settled."

"No." Valen pursed his lips. "Unfortunately, she won't have me."

"Izzie? You rejected his suit?" He frowned at his sister.

She slapped her hands to her side and huffed up her shoulders. "He brought no suit."

"I did," Valen answered evenly. "She said no."

"Well then," Robert took up his stance and poised his sword. "It must be done."

Valen climbed out of bed and took up the other sword.

Izzie held up both hands warding off her brother. "Are you mad? This is nonsense. He was wounded protecting me."

"Your honor is at stake, Izzie. It's my duty." Robert checked his feet and shook the sword to see how much play there was in the blade. "Unless you've reconsidered?"

Hands on hips. The marmot is vexed.

Valen gestured with his blade at her stance. "You see. She won't have me. Not plump enough in the pocket for her."

"This is absurd. He did not compromise me."

"I have witnesses. Father?"

Lord Ransley nodded gravely. "Saw it with my own eyes."

"Through a telescope you mean." She crossed her arms, and sulked in his father's direction.

Valen almost broke his concentration and smiled.

"Robert, you can't—" At last, Izzie was pleading.

Robert stuck to their plan and ignored her. "Are you ready, St. Cleve?"

"Yes. If will do me the service of wounding the same side. Wouldn't want both arms out of service, unless, of course, you feel you must take more drastic measures."

Robert moved his sword to the ready. "Don't know. How warm were those kisses?"

Izzie stepped between them and held up her hands to each of them. "No! You will stop this at once."

"A matter of honor." Valen nudged her aside with his hand and the guard of his sword. "Stand aside, Marmot."

"I will not. Robert, listen to me. It was one small kiss. Not nearly warm enough to merit a scratch."

Valen let his blade fall to the floor. "You crush me to the core, my lady. Your kisses certainly warmed me."

"Well, I . . ." She had the good grace to blush.

"And on several occasions," he added with enthusiasm.

Robert snorted angrily. "If this is true, Izzie, why the devil won't you marry him?"

Valen answered for her. "As I said—my lack of funds."

"It's that ridiculous plan of yours, is it?" Robert cradled his sword in his arms and frowned at her. "Still fancying yourself as Joan of Arc? Out to save the family." He shook his head. "Would you really do it, Izzie? Choose that Milquetoast Horton over St. Cleve?"

* * *

Elizabeth looked from Valen to her brother. Both had riveted their attention on her, intently awaiting her answer. Indeed, neither took a breath. And suddenly she comprehended their scheme.

"That's it, isn't it?" She turned to Lord Ransley, astounded. "Are you part of this conspiracy as well?"

Lord Ransley coughed and conveniently turned his head.

She inhaled deeply. "Well, it may interest all of you to know that I made this very decision days ago."

Their collective countenances were a gratifying assortment of shock and amazement.

The Red Hawk quickly recovered from his disadvantage, his eyes sharp and assessing. "And what, precisely, did you decide?"

He has no right to know, not after confronting me so meanly and trying to trick me into confessing my love for him.

Elizabeth stamped her foot, and fought to control her emotions, which meant of course elevating her chin. "A simple 'I love you, Lady Elizabeth, will you marry me?' would have sealed the bargain."

"You can't mean it!" Valen plopped down on the edge of the bed and pointed to his father. "You heard her." He turned back to Elizabeth baffled. "That day, when I explained to my father about how you refused me, you failed to express even the slightest regret—"

"That?" Elizabeth couldn't believe her ears. "*That* was supposed to win a profession of love out of me?"

"Well . . ." He hesitated, groping for words. "I was testing the waters . . . You didn't seem too . . ."

He slumped and winced because of it, straightening his back again to relieve the pain.

Valen got up, set his sword in its case, and took Elizabeth's shoulders in his hands. "So, am I given to understand you've had a change of heart?"

She nodded and smiled at him. "Almost since the moment we left the garden. Indeed, I could not escape my regret through this whole ordeal."

He answered with a broad grin and bent to kiss her.

Robert's sword came between them. "Here now. I would hate to have to call you out again."

Lady Alameda stood in the doorway. "Well, well, so our wily marmot has stopped bearing her claws and making a muddle of it, has she?"

Elizabeth was too happy to be completely annoyed, but she had to draw the line. "I do wish everyone would stop calling me that. I am convinced there is no such creature. A mythical invention—"

"Oh dear. What i*th* happening? Robert, deare*th*, why do you have your *th*word drawn?"

Elizabeth groaned and was just on point of demanding what the devil Miss Dunworthy was doing here, when Lady Alameda answered the question.

"Only look, Valen dearest, I have brought you some visitors. They were waiting downstairs until you and Robert concluded your *business*. Naturally, I thought you would be anxious to see Miss Dimworthy and her brother."

"Dunworthy," Elizabeth murmured.

Lady Alameda tilted her head as if considering the correction. "Oh, yes, so she has. Done quite well."

Robert set down his rapier and went to greet the paragon whose noodlelike curls were artfully arranged inside an adorable straw lace capote. "Lord Ransley, Lady Alameda, Lord St. Cleve, Elizabeth, allow me to present my betrothed, Miss—"

"Your what?" Elizabeth's hand went to her mouth to stifle the rest of her outcry.

Robert beamed proudly. "Miss Susannah Dunworthy has agreed to be my wife."

"She hasn't." Elizabeth's hands fell to her side and if Valen hadn't guided her to the edge of the bed so she might be seated, she might have collapsed to the floor. Luckily, Elizabeth was not the swooning type.

"She has, indeed." Robert patted his beloved's shoulders. "I warned her that I have nothing to offer her. Yet still, she would not say nay." He and the Miss Devious gazed into each other's eyes, and Elizabeth felt slightly queasy.

Miss Dunworthy smiled at all of them. "Indeed, my father was in *th*uch high alt over dear Robert'*th* devo*th*ion to me that he offered to pay all of his debts in addi*th*ion to my dowry. Dear Papa, he *th*inks only of my happine*th*."

Mr. Dunworthy didn't appear quite so convinced of this statement. While assessing the condition of his fingernails, he muttered, "Daresay, the future title didn't influence him at all."

Miss Dunworthy ignored her elder brother and rushed out of Robert's embrace to take Elizabeth's hands in her tiny little gloved palms. "*Th*ay you are happy for u*th*, Lady Eli*th*abeth." She smiled so hesitantly, as if she sincerely desired Elizabeth's approval and feared she might not win it, that Elizabeth was on point of opening her arms to the girl. But the little minx added, "I'm *th*ertain we will become the deare*th* of friends, you and I. We have *th*o mu*th* in common de*th*pite our great age differen*the*."

Lady Alameda clapped her hands together. "Isn't she adorable."

Some less than adorable descriptions rumbled around Elizabeth's ferocious marmot brain. Haughty rejoinders like: "Spiteful little mushroom." And "We shall be friends when the devil takes up crocheting . . ."

Fortunately, Valen, who must have been reading her mind, nudged her sharply in the ribs.

Elizabeth inhaled deeply and managed a smile. "I wish you both all the happiness in the world." And for Robert's sake, she meant every word. Elizabeth glanced at her twin, suddenly worried he had sacrificed himself as she had planned to do with Lord Horton. But an unfathomable glow of affection for his betrothed set Elizabeth's mind at ease. *He truly admires the girl.* She smiled at her brother.

He announced, "We will have the banns read for the first time next Sunday. We hope to marry in a fortnight or two."

"Lovely," Lady Alameda pronounced and motioned toward the door. "I'm certain we have wearied Lord St. Cleve. He must have his rest to recuperate. Let us retire to the great hall for some celebratory refreshments, tea and cakes. Champagne?"

No one seemed to notice that Elizabeth stayed behind. Lord Ransley was the last one to leave. "Bless you, my children." He took a joyful backward look, nodded at them, and shuffled off down the hall.

The room fell awkwardly silent. Valen reached for her hand. "Why did you not tell me?"

"What?" she chuckled. "And miss out on that astonishing performance."

"You might have spared me the embarrassment."

"I have been giving you hints all week."

"Those long heavy sighs?" A low rumble in his throat warned her of his skepticism. "I took those to mean any number of indecipherable sentiments. In the future, kindly use an alphabet I might comprehend. If I had known a simple statement would have resolved the matter—"

"Clearly, you preferred a more complicated solution."

"You realize, of course, that I do."

"Yes," she nodded. "You have a very complex mind."

"No." He grinned, quirking up his devilish dimples. "I do love you."

"Oh."

"So much so, I—" Valen glanced down at her fingers, toying with them. "When I thought I was dying, I could not bear the thought of never holding your hand again, never touching you. I regretted that I might never see the face of our son. Or . . ." He looked up with such yearning, Elizabeth's soul flew without hesitation off the roof and melted quite happily into his. "Elizabeth, marry me. I want you beside me when I wake up and when I lie down—"

Mythical creature, or not, marmots are not a particularly patient species. Elizabeth laid her hand on Valen's cheek and leaned forward to answer him with the warmest of kisses.

Author's Note

Medical practices in the Regency era were a fascinating blend of burgeoning science and cruel, almost torturous, traditions. On the battlefield, both French and British surgeons attempted to stop bleeding by bloodletting and applying leeches.

In one grisly account, a soldier was bled drastically following his surgery to reduce the blood flow. When surgeons still could not stop his bleeding, they applied twelve leeches to his wound. He awoke in agony, and, like our hero, plucked off the parasites and threw them. Amazingly, the soldier recovered, which is more a testament to his courage and fortitude than the medical care he received.

For more anecdotes about medical practices during the Regency era, and, if you have the stomach for it, a look at some of their actual surgical equipment, please visit my website: www.Kathleen Baldwin.com.

More Regency Romance
From Zebra